DANGEROUS DUKES

Rakes about town

Carole Mortimer introduces London's
most delectable dukes in her new miniseries.
But don't be fooled by their charm, because
beneath their lazy smiles, they're deliciously sexy—
and highly dangerous!

Coming this month
ZACHARY BLACK: DUKE OF DEBAUCHERY

And don't miss
DARIAN HUNTER: DUKE OF DESIRE
Available November 2014

"You have run out of time, I am afraid."

Zachary returned her gaze coldly as the carriage came to a stop outside Hawksmere House. "Perhaps you would care to come inside and finish the conversation there?"

Said the spider to the fly, Georgianna mentally added as she gave another shiver of apprehension. Being alone in this man's carriage with him had been more than a test for her nerves. Entering Zachary Black's home would push her well beyond her limits of daring.

What would he say or do if he were to learn exactly who she was? Would he shun her, as all of society now shunned her? Or would he exact the revenge she had long been waiting for?

Zachary Black, with his reputation as the coldly ruthless Duke of Hawksmere, was not an enemy any sane person would voluntarily wish upon themselves.

* * *

Zachary Black: Duke of Debauchery
Harlequin® Historical #1204—October 2014

Carole Mortimer

—

Zachary Black: Duke of Debauchery

 HARLEQUIN® HISTORICAL

Recycling programs
for this product may
not exist in your area.

ISBN-13: 978-0-373-29804-4

ZACHARY BLACK: DUKE OF DEBAUCHERY

Copyright © 2014 by Carole Mortimer

Printed in U.S.A.

HARLEQUIN®
™ www.Harlequin.com

Did you know that these novels are also available as ebooks? Visit www.Harlequin.com.

Carole Mortimer also writes for Harlequin Presents®!

To all of you, thank you for reading my books.

CAROLE MORTIMER

was born in England, the youngest of three children. She began writing in 1978, and has now written more than 150 books for Harlequin®. Carole has six sons: Matthew, Joshua, Timothy, Michael, David and Peter. She says, "I'm happily married to Peter Sr.; we're best friends, as well as lovers, which is probably the best recipe for a successful relationship. We live in a lovely part of England."

Chapter One

Late February, 1815, outside White's Club, London.

'What the—?' Zachary Black, the Duke of Hawksmere, came to an abrupt halt as he climbed into his carriage and noticed the shadowy figure already seated on the far side. The lantern inside was turned down low, preventing him from seeing if it was a man or woman who sat back in the shadows. 'Lamb?' He turned to look accusingly at his groom, silver eyes glittering in the soft glow of the flickering lamp.

The middle-aged man straightened to attention. 'She said as 'ow you was expecting 'er, your Grace,' he offered questioningly.

His intruder was a woman then, Zachary processed grimly. But certainly not one he had been expecting.

Unless…

He had just spent the evening and part of the night at his club with his four closest friends celebrating the forthcoming nuptials of one of them, Marcus Wilding, the Duke of Worthing, and his ladylove, Lady Julianna Armitage. Their wedding was due to take place later on today.

Zachary had briefly toyed with the idea of marriage himself the previous year, a decision forced upon him by the circumstances of his father's will. But his attempt to secure a wife had gone so disastrously wrong he was reluctant to repeat the experience. However, his cynicism did not prevent him from wishing Worthing well in the venture. Indeed, he had done so until almost dawn.

Which now caused Zachary to wonder if perhaps the woman in his carriage was a part of those wedding celebrations? Possibly a gift from Worthing? And perhaps each of Zachary's other three close friends would all find a similar present awaiting them in their own carriages?

Maybe so, but Zachary intended to remain cautious until convinced otherwise. The war with Napoleon might be over, and the Corsican currently incarcerated on Elba, but these were still dangerous times, and finding an unknown woman waiting for him in his carriage was certainly reason enough for him to stay on his guard.

'Hawksmere House, Lamb,' he instructed tersely as he climbed fully into the carriage and the door closed behind him. He took a seat across from the mysterious woman, placing his hat on the seat beside him as the carriage moved forward.

Zachary's sight had now adjusted enough to the gloom for him to note that the woman wore a black veil, one that covered her from her bonneted head to her booted toe. Such an effective covering prevented Zachary from being able to tell if she was old or young, fat or thin.

Deliberately so?

No doubt.

Zachary maintained his silence. This woman had sought him out, and therefore it was incumbent upon her to state her reasons for having done so.

To state whether she was friend or foe.

Georgianna's heart was beating wildly in her chest as she looked across the carriage at the silently watchful Zachary Black, the Duke of Hawksmere. A man, should he discover her identity, who had every reason to dislike her intensely. And rumour had it that the hard and cynical Zachary Black was a dangerous man when he disliked, intensely or otherwise.

Georgianna repressed a shiver as she straightened her spine before greeting him huskily, 'Your Grace.'

'Madam.' He gave a terse inclination of his head, his fashionably overlong hair appearing the blue-black of a raven's wing in the dimmed lighting. His silver eyes were narrowed in his aquiline face; his brows were dark over those pale and shimmering eyes. He had sharp blades for cheekbones above an uncompromising and sculptured mouth and stern jaw.

Georgianna's gaze was drawn down inexorably to the spot just beneath that arrogant jaw, to the livid scar visible above the white of his shirt collar. A wound so long and straight that it almost looked as if someone had attempted to cut his throat. Which had no doubt been the intention of the Frenchman wielding the sabre which had been responsible for the injury.

She repressed another shiver as she hastily returned her gaze to the dark and saturnine face above it. 'I realise my presence in your coach might be considered as an…an unorthodox way of approaching you.'

'That would surely depend upon your reason for being here,' he drawled softly.

Georgianna's gloved hands were clenched tightly together beneath the concealing shroud of her black veil. 'There is… I have important news I need to… to impart to someone I believe is an acquaintance of yours.'

The man seated opposite her in the carriage did not appear to move, his expression remaining as mockingly indifferent as ever, yet Georgianna nevertheless sensed a sudden, watchful tension beneath that indifference.

'Indeed?' he murmured dismissively.

'Yes.'

He raised those dark brows. 'Then I may assume you did not intrude upon my carriage with the intention of sharing my bed for what is left of the night?'

'Certainly not!' Georgianna pressed back in shock against the comfortably upholstered seat.

He continued to look at her with those narrowed and merciless silver eyes for several long seconds. 'Pity,' he finally drawled. 'A satisfying tumble would have been a fitting end to what has already been a most enjoyable evening. Pray tell, then, what is this important news you so urgently need me to impart to an acquaintance of mine? So important, it would seem, that you wilfully used subterfuge and lies with which to enter my carriage, rather than call upon my home during the daylight hours?' he prompted mockingly.

Now that she was face-to-face with Zachary Black, albeit with her own face obscured beneath the black veil, Georgianna was asking herself the same question.

At two and thirty, the arrogantly disdainful Duke of Hawksmere was a man she believed few would ever approach readily.

Admittedly, his prowess on the battlefield, with both sword and pistol, was legendary. His prowess in the bedchamber equally so. But he was also a gentleman rumoured to deal with both in the same cold and ruthless manner.

A coldness and ruthlessness, as Georgianna knew better than most, said to be frighteningly decisive.

So much so that she had no doubt that were he to identify her he would not hesitate to halt the carriage and toss her unceremoniously out into the street.

That he might still do so, of course.

She drew in a deep breath. 'It is rumoured, or more precisely I have reason to believe you have certain... connections? In government?'

Zachary remained lazily slouched on the plushly upholstered seat of his ducal carriage, his expression of mockery and boredom unchanging. But inwardly he was instantly on the alert, not caring for the way in which this woman had hesitated before questioning his connections.

It implied that she had some knowledge of his having worked as an agent for the Crown this past four years. Information which was certainly not public knowledge. Indeed, his endeavours in that area would be of little use if it were.

He gave a dismissive shrug. 'I have many acquaintances in the House, if that is what you are referring to.'

'We both know it is not.'

'Indeed?' Damn it, who was this woman?

A younger woman, from the light and breathless sound of her voice, and possibly unmarried if her shocked reaction to the suggestion she was here to share his bed was any indication. She also appeared educated from her accent and manner of speaking, although that veil still prevented him from knowing as to whether she was fair or dark, fat or thin.

Or what she knew of his connections in government.

'Yes,' she asserted firmly.

'I am afraid that you have me at something of a disadvantage, madam. While you claim to know a lot about me, I do not even know your identity,' Zachary dismissed coldly.

Georgianna doubted that the arrogantly assured Zachary Black had ever been at a disadvantage in his privileged life. Nor was he under one now, for this was his carriage, and their conversation one over which he ultimately held power. As he always held power over all who were allowed, or dared to, enter his privileged world.

A power, a proximity, that she frankly found overwhelming.

She had forgotten—chosen to forget?—that the duke was so immediate, and his personality so overwhelming, that he seemed to possess the very air about him. Air perfumed with the smell of good cigars and brandy, no doubt from the evening he had just spent at his club with his friends. There was an underlying hint of the sharp tang of lemons and an earthy, insidious aroma she could only assume to be that of the man himself.

Allowing her personal nervousness and dislike of the man to bedevil her now, after all she had gone through, was not going to help Georgianna's cause in the slightest.

'It is not necessary for you to know who I am for you to arrange for me to meet with one of those gentlemen,' she continued determinedly.

'That is for me to decide, surely?' The duke leisurely picked a speck of lint from the sleeve of his black evening jacket before he looked up and pinned her once again with those coldly glittering eyes. 'And why come to me on the matter? Why not simply make an appointment and impart this knowledge to one of those gentleman yourself?'

Georgianna's gaze lowered. 'Because I very much doubt any of them would agree to meet with a mere

woman. Not without the recommendation of someone such as yourself.'

'You underestimate the influence of your own sex,
madam,' Hawksmere drawled derisively.

'Do I?' Somehow Georgianna doubted that.

She had been barely nineteen ten months ago when
her own father had accepted on her behalf the offer
of marriage she had received from an influential and
titled gentleman, all without giving any consideration
as to whether or not Georgianna would be happy in
such a marriage.

Her now-deceased father, she reminded herself
dully, having learnt upon her return to England just
yesterday that her father had died nine months ago,
and in doing so making a nonsense of the anger she
had felt towards him in regard to that betrothal.

'I believe so, yes,' Hawksmere dismissed harshly.
'Either way, I am not in the habit of listening to news
imparted to me by unknown women—most especially one who feels it necessary to lie her way into
my presence—let alone recommending that anyone
else should do so.'

Georgianna had expected this distrust and cynicism from a man whom she knew allowed very few
people into his inner circle of intimates—the four
friends from his schooldays, also dukes, being the
exception. Those same four friends with whom she
knew he had just spent the evening and most of the
night.

'Who I am does not have any bearing on the veracity of the information I wish to impart,' she maintained stubbornly.

'In your opinion.'

'In the opinion of any patriot.'

Zachary Black raised a mocking brow at her vehemence. 'A patriot of what, madam?'

'Of England, of course.' Georgianna glared beneath the veil.

'Ah, yes, England,' he drawled drily. 'I trust you will forgive my ignorance, but I had thought England to currently be at peace? That we had held celebrations in honour of that peace just this past summer?'

'That is the very reason—' Georgianna broke off her outburst in order to draw in a deep and controlling breath. Being anything less than in control in this particular gentleman's company was not wise when he was more like than not to take advantage of it. 'I can trust in your discretion, I hope?'

He raised those mocking brows. 'Should that not have been something you ascertained before you decided to invade the privacy of my carriage?'

Yes, it should, and Georgianna had believed that she had done so; she would not have approached the Duke of Hawksmere if she had not known he was exactly the gentleman she needed to speak with initially.

And yet, alone with him now in his carriage, and presented with the perfect, and wholly private, opportunity in which to convince him into speaking on her behalf, she found herself hesitating.

To the country at large the Duke of Hawksmere was nothing less than a war hero. He'd fought bravely and long in Wellington's army and had been severely wounded for his trouble. That he had also worked secretly for the Crown was not so widely known, but just as heroic. It was Georgianna's personal dislike of the man which now caused her hesitation.

Alone with Hawksmere in his carriage, so totally overwhelmed by the sheer presence of the man, Georgianna could not help but be aware that he was also a man known for his ruthlessness.

Once again she straightened her shoulders as if for battle. 'You may pretend and posture all you like, your Grace, but I have no doubt that, once we have spoken a little longer, you will choose to speak on my behalf.'

Zachary would admit to being somewhat intrigued and not just by the information this young woman so urgently wished to impart. It was the woman herself who also interested him. Her voice might be young and educated, but it had also sounded slightly naïve when she stated her impassioned loyalty to England. Her claimed loyalty to England?

And Zachary still wondered what she looked like beneath that concealing veil.

Was she fair or dark? Beautiful or plain? Slender or rounded?

Zachary now found himself curious to know the answer to all of those questions. To see this young woman, if only so that he could look upon her face and judge for himself as to whether she spoke truthfully or otherwise. These last four years of working secretly for the Crown had shown him only too well not to trust anyone but his closest friends. How easily this could be an elaborate trap, a way of piquing his interest, before this mystery woman proceeded to feed the English government false information.

And his interest was most assuredly piqued.

To the extent that he no longer felt the least effect from the wine and brandy he had enjoyed with his friends earlier on.

So much so that he had no intentions of allowing this young woman to leave his carriage without first ascertaining exactly who she was and how she came to know things about him she should not have known.

He glanced out of the window to see that dawn was just starting to break over London's rooftops.

'Then might I suggest…' he turned back to the young woman, just able to discern the pale oval of her face beneath that veil now '…as we will reach my home in just a few minutes, that now might be as good a time as any for you to confide at least a little of that information?'

Her hands twisted together beneath that veil. 'I— It concerns the movements of a…a notable personage, currently residing on an island in the Mediterranean.'

It took every ounce of Zachary's considerable self-control not to react to this statement. Not to show, by so much as the twitch of an eyelid, that her information might be of interest him.

Who in hell was this woman?

And what exactly did she know?

He turned once again to look out of the window, as if bored by the conversation. 'As far as I am aware I do not have any acquaintances currently residing on a Mediterranean island.'

'I did not say he was a personal acquaintance of yours—'

'Then I cannot see what possible interest any of this can be to me,' Zachary cut her off harshly; even mentioning that the noble personage in question was a he could be dangerous.

Having chosen his servants himself, Zachary trusted them implicitly. But that did not mean he wished to test that trust by allowing any of them to overhear the details of his conversation with this woman and her implication that he was an agent for the Crown.

A young woman whose eyes now glittered across the width of the carriage at him from beneath that veil. Dark eyes. Brown or possibly a deep blue, he could not tell.

'I assure you, it will be of great interest to...'

'You have run out of time, I am afraid.' Zachary returned her gaze coldly as the carriage came to a stop outside Hawksmere House. 'Perhaps you would care to come inside and finish the conversation there?'

Said the spider to the fly, Georgianna mentally added as she gave another shiver of apprehension. Being alone in this man's carriage with him had been more than a test for her nerves. Entering Zachary Black's home with him would push her well beyond her limits of daring.

Although many might think otherwise, she acknowledged heavily, knowing her reputation was beyond repair as far as society was concerned. And most assuredly so in Hawksmere's cold and condemning gaze.

What would he say or do if he were to learn exactly who she was? Would he shun her, as all of society now shunned her? Or would he exact the revenge she had long been waiting for? That Sword of Damocles which she had felt balanced above her head for so many months now.

Zachary Black, with his reputation as the coldly ruthless Duke of Hawksmere, was not an enemy any sane person would voluntarily wish upon themselves.

And yet Georgianna had done so.

And done so willingly at the time, in the belief that she had no other choice in the matter. It had only been in the months since that she'd had time to reflect, as well as deeply regret, her previous actions. To appreciate exactly what manner of man it was she had chosen to make her mortal enemy.

After just a few minutes spent in the company of Hawksmere, and being made totally aware of the dangerous edge beneath his smooth urbanity, was enough to confirm that he was the type of man who would never forget a slight or an insult.

And Georgianna had insulted him most grievously.

'I think not, thank you,' she now answered him coolly.

'I really wish you had answered differently.'

Georgianna was not fooled for a moment into thinking that Hawksmere's words of regret were because he was still under the misapprehension she was a lady of the night and he wished to bed her. His tone had been too unemotional, too calmly conversational, for that to be true.

She pressed back against the shadows of the carriage as the groom opened the door and the duke rose to his feet before stepping down on to the cobbled road, placing his hat upon his head before turning to hold out a hand to her.

'Our conversation is far from over,' he murmured pointedly as she made no attempt to take that hand.

'If you will just agree to speak to—speak on my behalf, your Grace,' she corrected as he frowned darkly, 'then I will return in a day or so for your answer. For now I choose to wait here a few minutes longer, before quietly leaving. I believe it preferable if we were not seen leaving the Hawksmere ducal carriage together.'

He raised one dark and mocking brow as he turned from dismissing the listening groom. 'Are you perhaps under the misapprehension that your preferences are of any interest to me?'

'On the contrary, I am sure they are not.' Georgianna continued to press back into the shadows. 'I was thinking of your own reputation rather than my own.'

Hawksmere gave a humourless smile. 'I am informed by my closest friends that my reputation is that of a gambler and an irredeemable rake.'

And Georgianna now believed that to be a reputation this man had deliberately fostered, as a way of diverting attention from the fact that he worked secretly as a spy for the Crown.

Oh, he was also undoubtedly both a gambler and a womaniser. He had more than enough funds to accommodate a liking for the former and both the arrogance and dangerous attraction to ensure he could satisfy the latter. He could surely have any woman who might come to the attention of those piercing silver eyes.

Well, almost any woman, Georgianna reminded herself, knowing that one woman, at least, had escaped the attentions of both that silver gaze and the man himself.

'No doubt you are,' she conceded softly. 'I would nevertheless still prefer to remain in the carriage until you are safely inside the house.'

Zachary was not a man known for his patience. Or his forbearance. Or, indeed, any of those admirable qualities that made certain gentlemen of the *ton* so acceptable to both the young débutantes and their marriage-minded mamas. The opposite, in fact; he and his four closest friends had earned the sobriquet The Dangerous Dukes amongst the *ton* this past ten years or more, and one of the reasons for that had been because they were none of them amiable or obliging. Or in the least interested in marrying any of those irritatingly twittering young women who appeared year after boring year on the marriage mart.

Zachary's brief flirtation with the idea of marriage had been out of necessity rather than inclination, his father's will demanding that he be married and have an heir by the time he reached the age of thirty-five, or forfeit the bulk of the Hawksmere fortune. The scandalous end to that betrothal meant that Zachary had delayed repeating the experience as yet. Although, now aged two and thirty, he appreciated that his time was assuredly running out, and he would soon be forced to once again take his pick of the Season's beauties.

Worthing was to marry later on today, of course, but as he was to marry the younger sister of another of The Dangerous Dukes, it did not signify; the beautiful Julianna Armitage was neither twittering nor irritating.

So far in their acquaintance, Zachary had not found the earnest young woman behind the black veil to be either of those things either, though.

'You consider I am in some danger, then?' he enquired mildly. 'From yourself, perhaps?'

'Certainly not,' she gasped. 'I assure you, I did not come here to cause you any more harm—' She broke off abruptly even as she seemed to cringe even further back against the carriage seat.

'More harm?' Zachary's eyes narrowed even as he leant forward until his shoulders filled the doorway of the carriage, his gaze searching on that veiled figure. 'Who are you?' he prompted harshly.

'I am no one, your Grace.'

'On the contrary, you are most certainly someone.' He reached into the ever-lightening gloom of the carriage to grasp one of her arms before pulling her along the seat towards him. A soft and slender arm that answered at least one of his earlier questions; the young woman beneath the veil was slender, very much so.

'Let me go.' She struggled against his hold, her gloved hand moving up in an effort to try to prise his fingers from about her arm. 'You must release me, your Grace.' There was now a distressed sob in her voice as her attempts failed to secure her release.

'I think not,' Zachary said slowly.

It had never been his intention to just allow this young woman to leave. Not since she had mentioned having information on Bonaparte, not by name but by implication.

Besides which, his curiosity to know more about this woman had only deepened with her comment about inflicting more harm.

The implication surely being that she had caused him some personal harm in the past?

If that was the case, then Zachary intended to know exactly who she was and in what way she might have caused him harm.

To that end he leant inside the carriage and pulled her easily towards him, until she fell forward across his shoulder despite her struggles.

'What are you doing?'

'I should have thought that was obvious.' Zachary backed out of the carriage before straightening to heft his feather-light burden more comfortably on to his shoulder, his arm tight about the backs of the young woman's thighs. He shot the curiously observing Lamb a grimly satisfied grin as he stood beside the horses' heads, holding the reins to keep them steady. 'The lady has expressed a fancy to pretend she is being kidnapped by a lusty pirate and carried off to his lair.'

Georgianna gave an indignant squeak at the deliberate and mortifying fabrication, before turning appealingly to the stoic-faced groom. 'Do not believe a word of it,' she pleaded desperately, the blood having rushed to her head and now causing her to feel slightly dizzy. 'I am certainly being kidnapped, but not by any lusty pirate.'

'Quiet, wench.' The Duke of Hawksmere gave her a hearty slap on her backside to accompany the piratical instruction. 'Wish me luck with my plundering, Lamb,' he added drily, 'for I am certain I shall need it.'

'Not you, your Grace.' The groom grinned his enjoyment of the entertainment. 'Women are much like feisty mares and I've never known of one of 'em as you couldn't tame to the bridle.'

Georgianna's cheeks were aflame with colour, her light-headedness giving the whole situation a dreamlike quality. One in which she felt like the spectator at a theatre farce.

What other explanation could there possibly be for the way she now dangled over one of the wide and muscled shoulders of Zachary Black, the dangerous Duke of Hawksmere?

To now be jostled and bounced as he carried her up the steps of his town house, through the open doorway, before taking the three-pronged and lit candelabrum from the surprised and haughty-faced butler into his other hand?

The duke continued on through the entrance hall before taking the steps two at a time as he carried Georgianna easily up the wide staircase to the bed-chambers above.

Chapter Two

'Remove the veil.' Zachary looked down grimly at the young woman he had just seconds ago dropped unceremoniously on top of the covers on his four-poster bed. The lit candelabrum he had placed on the bedside table allowed him to see the way her petticoat and the skirt of her black gown rode up and revealed slender and shapely ankles. Catching him looking, she hastily pulled the garments down again. Unfortunately that concealing veil had remained irritatingly in place. 'Now,' he ordered uncompromisingly.

Georgianna looked up warily through her long lashes at her towering adversary as she scrabbled further up the bed, as far away from the ominously threatening Duke of Hawksmere as it was possible for her to be. 'I have no intentions of removing my veil.'

'Are you in mourning?'

Was she? Her father had certainly died in the past year, but even so that was not her reason for wearing the veil.

'If you have to think about it, then obviously not,' the duke dismissed coldly. 'Remove the veil. Now. Before I lose what little patience I have left,' he added warningly.

Georgianna's response to Hawksmere's dangerously soft voice was to sit up straighter in the lush pile of snowy white pillows at the head of the four-poster bed. 'You cannot treat me in this high-handed manner.'

'No?' His tone was low and menacing. 'I do not see anyone rushing to your rescue.'

Her cheeks flamed with heat as she continued to look at him from beneath lowered lashes. 'That is because you told your groom... Because your servants now think...'

'That I am continuing to play my part in your erotic fantasy and am now ravishing you?' Hawksmere completed derisively.

'Yes.'

The duke gave a grimly satisfied smile. 'And can you tell me truthfully that you have never had such a fantasy? That you have never dreamed,' he added, sensually soft, 'of a swashbuckling pirate carrying you off to his ship before having his wicked way with you?'

Of course Georgianna had once had such fantasies. What young and romantic girl had not dreamed of being carried off and ravished by a wicked pirate, or perhaps a dashing knight, who would then fall instantly in love with her and keep her for ever?

But she was now twenty years of age and felt much

older than that in her heart. Nor did she have any faith left in romance and love. She knew only too well that the reality did not match up to the fantasy, that the wicked pirate or the dashing knight invariably had feet of clay.

'Those are the daydreams of silly young girls who do not know any better,' she dismissed flatly.

'And you do?'

'Oh, yes,' she assured with feeling.

Hawksmere's lids lay heavy over his eyes as he smiled down at her mockingly. 'In that case, might I suggest you stop behaving like the ridiculous heroine in a lurid novel and remove your veil?'

Georgianna did not see that she had any choice in the matter when the duke was so much bigger than she was and could so obviously force her to his will if he so chose. And his mocking assertions earlier as to his reason for bringing her to his bedchamber meant she could not expect to receive any assistance from Hawksmere's servants, either.

She had, Georgianna now realised, placed herself completely at the duke's mercy.

And those cold silver eyes, and the uncompromising set of his arrogant jaw, confirmed that this man gave no quarter, to man or woman.

She slowly raised her shaking hands to where the pins held the veil in place. 'You will not like what you see,' she warned as she slowly began to remove those pins.

Hawksmere raised dark brows. 'Are you disfigured in some way? From the pox, perhaps?'

'No.' She sighed as she placed the pins on the night table beside the candelabrum of three flickering candles.

'Ugly, then?' he dismissed uninterestedly. 'Something my bedchamber has certainly not seen before.'

And such a richly ornate bedchamber it was, too, and entirely fitting for a duke as wealthy and powerful as Hawksmere. The curtains at the windows and about the four-poster bed were of a rich blue velvet and the furniture was heavy and dark and at the height of fashion. A thick, predominantly blue Aubusson carpet almost entirely covered the floor while a cheery fire burned in the large, ornate fireplace.

The room was almost as magnificent as the duke himself, attired as he was in tailored evening clothes of black jacket and breeches, and waistcoat of fine silver brocade, his linen snowy white, a diamond pin glinting in the neckcloth at his throat.

The same magnificent duke whose mistresses were rumoured to be some of the most beautiful women in the land.

'I am neither ugly nor beautiful, I am merely a woman.' Georgianna's hands trembled even more as she began to remove the concealing black veil.

'Then I fail to see what it is you believe I shall dis—' Zachary stopped talking as the veil came off completely and he was able to look at the woman's face for the first time.

She had lied to him because she was most certainly beautiful. Very much so. Her hair was raven-black beneath her bonnet, equally black and shapely above eyes hidden by the lowering of the longest, darkest lashes he had ever seen, her nose short and straight. Best of all was her magnificent mouth, the lips full and pouting, and surely meant for a man to kiss and devour? And other, much more carnal delights.

That was Zachary's first thought. His second was something else entirely as he eyed that pale face, that delicious mouth, in frowning concentration. 'Do I know you?'

Georgianna almost choked over the hysterical laughter that rose in her throat, at having Zachary Black, of all men, ask if he knew her.

If he knew her?

Not only was it highly insulting to have him look at her with such quizzical half recognition, but it also made a complete mockery of her having bothered to wear the black veil as a disguise in the first place; she had fully expected this man to take one look at her and remember exactly how, and why, he knew her.

'Perhaps if you were to cast your mind back to last April, your Grace, it might help to jolt your memory?' she prompted sarcastically.

'Last April?' Zachary's lids narrowed as he studied her more closely. 'Take off your bonnet,' he ordered harshly.

Her brows lowered as she looked up at him for the first time without that concealing veil and revealing deep blue eyes, the colour of violets in springtime.

Unforgettably beautiful eyes, even if the rest of this woman's appearance, apart from that tempting mouth, had changed beyond all recognition.

If this young woman was indeed whom Zachary suspected she might be, then the last time he had seen her she had been plump as a pigeon and stood only an inch or two over five feet in height. She'd rosy, rounded cheeks, ample breasts spilling over the top of her gown, and curvaceous hips a man would enjoy grasping on to as he parted those plump thighs and thrust deep inside her.

She now appeared so slender that a puff of wind might blow her away. Indeed, Zachary knew from carrying her up the stairs that she weighed no more than a child of ten. Her skin was very pale against the black gown buttoned up to her throat, her breasts small, waist and thighs slender, as were the shapely calves and ankles he had glimpsed earlier.

She sighed. 'I am growing a little tired of your instructions, Hawksmere.'

'And I am beyond tired of your delay,' he returned angrily.

'Perhaps if you were to consider using the word please occasionally, especially when addressing a woman, you might meet with more co-operation to your requests?' She reached up slender hands to untie the ribbon beneath her pointed chin.

Zachary's hands were now clenched so tightly into fists at his sides that he knew he was in danger of the short fingernails piercing the skin. 'I reserve such politeness for women who have not invaded my carriage by the use of falsehood and lies. Now, remove the damned bonnet.'

Georgianna knew from the violence in Hawksmere's tone that she had now pushed him to the limit of his patience. Perhaps beyond that limit, for those silver eyes glittered dangerously in that harshly handsome face, his hands clenching and unclenching at his sides as if he were resisting the urge to reach out and place them about her throat before squeezing tightly.

If he had finally recognised her, then she had no doubt that was exactly how he felt.

Georgianna glared up at him defiantly as she finally removed the offending bonnet, revealing thick, ebony curls secured at her crown, a shorter cluster of curls at her temple, and the slender nape of her neck.

'Well, well, well.' Hawksmere gave a predatory smile, that silver gaze remaining on Georgianna's face as he began to pace slowly at the foot of the bed. His sleek and muscled body seemed to flow with the dangerous grace of the predator he now resembled. 'If it is not Lady Georgianna Lancaster come to call. Or perhaps I should now be addressing you as Madame Rousseau?' he added scornfully.

Leaving Georgianna in no doubt that this man, Zachary Black, the arrogant Duke of Hawksmere, now knew exactly who she was.

She felt the colour leach from her cheeks, her heart once again beating erratically in her chest, as she saw how the duke's silver eyes glittered with a cold, remorseless, and utterly unforgiving anger.

An anger that turned to scathing satisfaction as he saw the answer to his question in her now-ravaged expression. 'So your gallant Frenchman did not marry you, after all, but merely settled for having you warm his bed,' he stated mockingly as he ceased his pacing and suddenly lowered his lean and muscled length into the chair beside the ornate fireplace, those devil's eyes never leaving Georgianna's deathly pale face for a moment.

An icy coldness settled in Georgianna's chest. Her limbs felt heavy with fatigue, her lips so numb she doubted she would be able to speak even if she tried.

But she did not try; she knew that she deserved whatever scorn Hawksmere now chose to shower upon her head.

However, being carried so unceremoniously up to the duke's bedchamber and forced to reveal her identity was not supposed to have happened.

She had intended to meet Hawksmere in the darkness of his carriage, under the guise of anonymity, making her request for him to arrange for her to speak to someone in government, before fading into shadowed obscurity as she awaited an answer to that request. Fully aware it was all she could expect from Hawksmere, following the events of ten months ago.

'And is your French gallant here in England with you?' Hawksmere now prompted softly.

Georgianna drew in a steadying breath. 'You must know that he is not.'

He raised dark brows. 'Must I?'

She blinked back the sting of tears in her eyes. 'Do not play cat-and-mouse games with me, your Grace, when I have no defences left with which to withstand your cruelty.'

Zachary felt cruel. More than cruel. Despite his

outward calm, he had an inner longing to punch something. Someone. To take out his anger, his frustration with this situation, on living, breathing flesh.

Oh, not Georgianna Lancaster's tender flesh, of course; he had never hit a woman in his life, and as deserved as the anger he felt towards her might be, he was not about to start now by so much as placing a finger upon that smooth alabaster skin.

For, unlikely as it might seem, it truly was her, Zachary acknowledged incredulously as he continued to study her through narrowed lids. And he could surely be forgiven for not having recognised her immediately, when she was so much paler and more slender than she had been a year ago. When those beautiful eyes no longer brimmed over with a love of life.

With love for her erstwhile French lover?

If that was true, then, she had got exactly what she deserved, Zachary dismissed coldly. Disillusionment. Betrayal.

Unless…

'When did it become obvious to you that your lover was not the French *émigré* he claimed to be when he came to take up residence in England, but was actually a spy sent here by Napoleon himself?' Zachary channelled his anger into biting words rather than physical retribution. 'That his name was not Duval at all, but Rousseau?'

She bowed her head. 'Not soon enough.' The tears spilt unchecked over those long dark lashes before falling down her pale and hollow cheeks.

Not soon enough.

Zachary knew exactly what that meant. 'Did he ever have any intention or marrying you, do you think?' he scorned. 'Or was it his plan all along to just use you to hide his true identity?'

'What a truly hateful man you are.' Georgianna buried her face in her hands as the hot tears fell in earnest, sobbing brokenly at the same time as she knew that she wholly deserved Hawksmere's anger and his scorn. His disgust.

For she truly was a disgrace. That romantic fool whom Hawksmere had described earlier.

A young and romantic fool who had believed André loved her, that they were running away together, eloping, in order to be married. That he'd acted as her saviour, rescuing her from the prospect of a loveless marriage. Only for her to discover, once they reached a chaotic Paris, the city still in turmoil following Napoleon's surrender, that her lover had never had any intentions of marrying her.

Something André had wasted no time in revealing once he was safely back in France. Their elopement, he had told her, had acted only as a foil; as a way of hiding his real reason for fleeing England so suddenly and returning to his native France.

Something she felt sure that Hawksmere, as a spy for the Crown, must surely now be aware of. Not because he had any interest in learning what had become of her, but because André and his fellow conspirators—Bonapartists—were men whom England needed to watch.

'How you personally feel towards me has no bearing on the importance of the information I have brought back with me from France,' she now assured the duke dully.

'France?'

'Yes.'

Hawksmere shrugged those wide shoulders, elbows on the arms of the chair in which he sat, his fingers steepled together in front of his devilishly handsome face.

'Information which must surely be tainted by the mere fact that your word is not to be trusted. That you might now be a spy yourself, come to give the English government false information on your lover's behalf.'

Geogianna's eyes widened at the accusation. 'I told you I am a loyal subject of England.'

'One who has willingly been living in France with her lover this past ten months.'

'I have not seen or spoken to André Rousseau for many of those months,' Georgianna denied heatedly.

At first she had been too ill to leave France; once recovered, there had been no money to enable her to leave, even if she had wanted to. Which in reality she had not, knowing herself to be unwelcome in England after disgracing her whole family, as well as herself, in the eyes of society.

A family she was sure must have disowned her completely following her elopement with André.

So, yes, she had remained in France, all the time keeping her ears and eyes open to the plots and plans that so abounded in the streets, the shops, and the taverns of the city. Plots to liberate Napoleon from the Mediterranean island of Elba, where he now reigned as emperor of just twelve thousand souls.

Which, she reminded herself determinedly, was the only reason why she would ever have deliberately sought the company of the Duke of Hawksmere.

'No?' The duke eyed her mockingly.

'I gave you my word.'

'And I, of all people, have good reason to doubt your every word, Georgianna.'

She sighed. 'Your distrust of me is understandable.'

'It is kind of you to say so,' Hawksmere drawled with obvious sarcasm.

A flush warmed her cheeks at the deserved rebuke. 'I am well aware that I wronged you.'

'You wronged and disgraced yourself, madam, not me.' Zachary stood up restlessly to stride over to the window and look out into the park below as he wondered if such a strange and ridiculous situation as this had ever existed before.

Here he was, the powerful Duke of Hawksmere, fêted and fawned upon by the elite of the *ton* and society as a whole, alone in his bedchamber with Lady Georgianna Lancaster, a woman who had behaved so disgracefully in the past that if it were publically known, he doubted society would ever open its doors to her again.

A young woman whom Zachary had good reason to believe would never enter his bedchamber, under any circumstances.

And she had not come willingly this time, either, he reminded himself, but she'd been carried up here, thrown over his shoulder with no more concern than if she had been a sack of coal, her indignant protests at his actions completely ignored.

Because Zachary had not known who she was at the time, could have no idea that it was Georgianna Lancaster hiding beneath that veil and bonnet.

And if he had?

Would he have behaved any differently if he had known of her identity?

That identity, her history and association with André Rousseau, would have made it impossible for Zachary to simply ignore her. Or the information she said she had come here to impart.

'I apologise for my past wrongs to you.'

'I have absolutely no interest in your apologies, Georgianna, in the past or now,' Zachary assured her scathingly as he turned back to face her, his cool expression masking the shock he once again felt at the changes these past ten months had wrought in her.

Georgianna Lancaster's face was now ghostly pale rather than rosy as a freshly picked apple. Her violet eyes now dark and haunted, her alabaster skin stretching tautly over the delicacy of the bones at her cheeks and throat and her figure wraith-thin.

Because, as she claimed, she had been seduced, before then being abandoned by her French lover?

Or because of the nervousness of possibly days or weeks spent considering the enormity of the deception she was about to practise on her lover's behalf?

Zachary was wary and cynical enough to know that the rift that apparently now existed between Georgianna Lancaster and André Rousseau could all just be a ruse. And that she might have only returned to England to carry out her lover's instructions of passing along false information to the English government.

Until Georgianna revealed the full details of that information, Zachary had no way of knowing what was true and what was not.

Georgianna raised her chin, determined that Zachary Black should hear her out. Whether he wished it or not. The cold mockery in those glittering silver eyes, which now looked down at her so disdainfully, conveyed that he did not.

Her own eyes lowered so that she no longer had to look at that disdain. 'I have information.'

'Well?' he prompted hardly as she hesitated.

'It is Bonaparte's intention to leave Elba shortly and return to France as emperor.'

He shrugged wide shoulders. 'There have been rumours of his escaping Elba since he was first exiled there.'

'Oh,' Georgianna murmured flatly before rallying. 'But this time it is true.'

'So you say.'

Her eyes widened in alarm at the boredom of his tone. 'You have to believe me.'

'My dear Lady Georgianna, I do not have to do anything where you are concerned,' the duke assured softly as he crossed the bedchamber on stealthy feet, until he once again stood beside the bed on which she still sat. 'What were your lover's instructions regarding what you should do next, I wonder?' he prompted conversationally as he sat down on the bed beside her. 'If met with resistance from me, were you to then attempt to seduce me in order to gain my trust?'

Georgianna could only stare at him with wide and apprehensive eyes as he now sat so dangerously close to her his muscled thighs were just inches from her own. Close enough she could feel the heat of his immense body, smell the clean scent of lemon and sandalwood and that hint of the brandy and cigars he had enjoyed during the hours spent at his club earlier tonight.

So close that she could now see the black circle that rimmed those silver irises looking down at her so disdainfully. She noted the tautness of the flesh across aristocratic cheekbones. The top one of those sculptured lips curled back with the haughty disgust he so obviously felt towards her. That livid scar upon his throat a warning to all of how dangerous this gentleman could be.

As if to confirm that danger he gave a slow and sensuous smile.

'Feel free to begin any time you wish, Georgianna.'

Her alarm deepened at the cold mockery she saw in those hard silver eyes looking at her so contemptuously. 'I have no intention of attempting to seduce you.'

'No?' he drawled. 'Pity. It might at least have

proved amusing to see just how much your French lover has taught you this past year.'

'I told you, I have not so much as spoken to André in months.'

'And I am expected to believe that claim?' the duke drawled. 'To accept your word?' His jaw tightened, a nerve pulsing beside that livid scar at his throat. 'I am to accept the word of a woman whom I am only too well aware does not know the meaning of the word honour, let alone trust?'

Georgianna flinched at the icy dismissal of his tone. 'I was very young and foolish when you knew me last.'

'It was only ten months ago,' he cut in harshly. 'Am I now to accept that you have changed so much in that short time? That your word can now be trusted? The word of a woman who did not hesitate to cause disgrace to her family and herself just months ago in her desperation to elope with her French lover?'

Each deserved and hurtful word was like a whip lashing across Georgianna's flesh. Her eyes flooded anew with stinging tears, her body quivering at the landing of each successive and precise blow to her sensitised flesh.

She gave a weary shake of her head, unheeding of the tears still falling hotly down her cheeks. 'I am asking you to accept that the information I bring is completely removed from my own behaviour. That it is most urgent, even imperative, that you believe me when I tell you it is Bonaparte's intention to leave Elba soon and take up arms once again.'

'When, precisely?'

Her gaze dropped from meeting his. 'If you could arrange for me to speak with someone…'

'You do not trust me with this information?' He raised incredulous brows.

'Forgive me, but I have learnt this past ten months not to trust anyone completely,' she answered dully.

Zachary studied her between narrowed lids, hardening his heart to the tears that still lay upon those pale and hollowed cheeks. He reminded himself that this was the woman who had thought nothing of deceiving her own father, and the man who was to have been her husband, in order to run away with the Frenchman who was her younger brother's tutor.

It might be true that she had not seen André Rousseau for some months. Just as it might also be true that Georgianna Lancaster's unmarried state meant that she had reason to regret ever having eloped with the Frenchman in the first place.

But it might be just as true that this was all just a ruse and that she had been sent here by that lover to deceive and mislead the English government.

If the first of those things was true, then it was of no personal concern to Zachary; the woman had made her choices and must now live with them. No, it was the little information Georgianna Lancaster had already imparted, in regard to Napoleon's intention to soon leave Elba, which interested him.

For no matter what he might have said to Georgianna Lancaster, no rumour of Napoleon leaving Elba was ever ignored.

His nostrils flared.

'And I have no intention of so much as telling anyone of your presence back in England until I am satisfied you have told me all that you know.'

'Please.'

'Poor, bewildered Georgianna,' Zachary mocked the pained expression on her beautiful face as he slowly lifted his hand to gather up one of her tears on to his fingertip, looking down curiously at that tear before allowing it to fall to the carpeted floor at his feet as his gaze returned to her face. 'Did you really imagine it would be so easy to convince me of your sincerity? That I would listen to your information, be so concerned by it that I would then immediately arrange for you to speak to someone in the government?'

She swallowed. 'You must.'

'I have already told you I must do nothing where you are concerned, Georgianna,' Zachary thundered before quickly regaining control of his temper. A control he lost rarely, if ever. Testament, no doubt, to the anger he still harboured towards this woman. 'What have you really been doing these past ten months, I wonder?' he mused grimly.

She blinked. 'I told you, after André— Once I learnt he had merely been using me, I had no choice but to leave him.'

Zachary was fully aware that her violet gaze could no longer meet his own. A sure sign that she was lying? 'And what did you do then?' he prompted. 'How did you continue to live in France, Georgianna, with no money and, as you claim, no lover's bed to warm you?'

'It is not just a claim.'

'I am afraid that it is.'

Georgianna looked up at the duke apprehensively, not fooled for a moment by the calm evenness of his tone. 'What do you mean?'

He returned her gaze contemptuously. 'I mean that you have made a mistake in claiming Rousseau would ever have allowed you to leave him.'

Georgianna ran the tip of her tongue across suddenly dry lips before speaking huskily. 'Why do you say that?'

He gave a derisive laugh. 'My dear Georgianna, if you really were just the foolish romantic you claim to be, then once your usefulness to Rousseau was at an end he would have had no choice but to kill you for what you already knew about him, rather than simply allowing you to leave.'

She drew her breath in sharply, the colour draining from her cheeks even as she felt the burning in her chest and temple, a painful reminder that André had attempted to do exactly that.

She still cringed at the numbing disillusionment, the cruel and frightening way in which she had discovered André had never cared for her, but had merely been using her. And the shock, the devastation of learning that André intended to rid himself of the nuisance of her by taking her out of the city before killing her.

That he had not succeeded in doing so had been more by chance than deliberate intent.

And Georgianna had the scars, physical as well as emotional, to prove it.

Zachary remained unmoved by the haunted expression on Georgianna Lancaster's suddenly deathly pale face. Her elopement with André Rousseau, the mystery of where she had been and what she had been doing this past ten months, were all more than enough reason for him to distrust every word that came out of her delectable mouth.

And he did still consider it a delectably sensual mouth, he conceded regretfully. The sort of mouth that he had once imagined doing wild and wonderful things to his body—

Zachary stood up abruptly. 'Fortunately, the decision as to the truth, or otherwise, of the information you wish to impart, does not rest with me.'

'Then with whom?'

Zachary looked down at her grimly. 'There are others—less gentle than myself—who will decide the matter.'

'I do not understand.'

'You will, Georgianna.' Zachary hardened his heart to the increased bewilderment in those violet-coloured eyes. 'Have no doubt, you most certainly will.'

She stared up at him with fearful eyes. 'You cannot mean to— You are saying I shall be tortured, in order to ascertain whether or not I am telling the truth?'

'The English government does not resort to torture, Georgianna.' Zachary bared his teeth in a hard and mocking smile. 'Not openly, at least,' he added softly.

'You are trying to frighten me,' she accused emotionally.

'Am I succeeding?' he taunted.

'You must know that you are.' Her slender fingers tightly gripped one of the downy pillows.

'Poor Georgianna,' Zachary drawled mockingly. 'Are you even aware of your father's death?' he prompted sharply.

'Yes. I learnt of it yesterday when I returned to England.' Her lashes lowered. 'I— Do you have any news of Jeffrey?'

'He is well, I believe. Inheriting the title put paid to Cambridge, of course,' he drawled dismissively. 'But he fares well with his new responsibilities as Earl of Malvern, with the aid of his guardian.'

'Who on earth…?'

'I am sure your belated concern for your brother is all well and good, Georgianna,' Zachary continued dismissively, 'but it will not succeed in deflecting me, and others, from the suspicion that you might also now be a spy for Napoleon.' He gave a mocking shake of his head. 'And to think, just ten months ago the situation was all so very different. That if you had not run away, then all of this might now be yours.'

All of this, Georgianna knew, being the Hawksmere houses and estates, the title of duchess, and the Duke of Hawksmere himself as her husband.

All of which would most assuredly have been hers,

if she had continued with the betrothal her father had accepted on her behalf and married Zachary Black, the aloof and enigmatic Duke of Hawksmere.

It was every young girl's dream, of course, to receive an offer of marriage from a duke, to become his duchess, revered and looked up to by society.

It might also have been Georgianna's dream, too, if her father had once consulted her and not instead roused her stubbornness by accepting Hawksmere's offer without so much as discussing it with her.

If she had truly believed she could bear to be married to such a cold and arrogant man as Hawksmere, a man she had no doubt did not love her.

If she, stupid romantic fool that she had been, had not already believed herself to be madly in love with another man, a penniless tutor, whose situation in life had appealed to her young and too-innocent heart. The man she had believed to be in love with her.

As opposed to this man, Zachary Black, the icily composed Duke of Hawksmere, whom she knew had not loved her, but had only offered for her because she was the eminently suitable, and malleable, nineteen-year-old daughter of the Earl of Malvern.

Chapter Three

Georgianna had been flattered but terrified when her father first came to her and proudly told her of the offer of marriage he had received, and already accepted, on her behalf, from the wealthy and powerful Duke of Hawksmere.

Until that moment Hawksmere had been a gentleman Georgianna had never so much as spoken to and seen only rarely, and then only from a distance, at several of the *ton*'s entertainments during the past two Seasons. The toplofty gentleman had much preferred his clubs, and the company of his close friends, to the bustle and formality of society's much tamer entertainments.

But even viewed from a distance, Hawksmere had seemed intimidating to her, and aged one and thirty years to her nineteen, their twelve years' difference was so obvious in experience as well as age.

His demeanour was always one of icy disdain as he habitually looked down his arrogant nose at the crush of guests assembled at those entertainments. And the terrible scar visible upon the duke's throat had caused Georgianna to tremble every time she so much as glanced at it, as she imagined the raw savagery that must have been behind such an injury.

The very idea of her ever becoming the wife of such a haughtily cold and frightening gentleman had filled her young and romantic heart with fear. Especially so when the two of them had not so much as spoken a word to each other. Indeed, the only possible reason Georgianna could think of for the proposal was that, as the only daughter of the Earl of Malvern, Hawksmere must consider her a suitable candidate to provide his future heirs.

The dukedom aside, even the thoughts of the intimacy necessary to provide those heirs with such a terrifying man as Hawksmere had been enough to cause Georgianna's heart to pound fearfully in her chest.

Besides which, she was already in love and had been so for several months. With André Duval, the handsome and charming blond-haired, blue-eyed French *émigré* her father had taken pity on and brought into their home, so that he might help to prepare her younger brothe,r Jeffrey, for his entry into Cambridge.

That same handsome and charming blond-haired, blue-eyed Frenchman who just weeks later had so unemotionally taken her out to a wood outside Paris with the intention of killing her.

Tears of humiliation now burned Georgianna's

eyes as she looked up at Hawksmere. 'As I said, I was very young and very foolish,' she said dully.

'And now you are so much older and wiser,' Hawksmere taunted.

'Yes.' Georgianna's eyes flashed darkly. This man could have no idea of how much older and wiser she was, how much even a loveless marriage to him would have been preferable to the fate that had befallen her.

He eyed her pityingly. 'I trust you will forgive me when I say I do not believe you?'

'I very much doubt that you have ever needed anyone's forgiveness, least of all mine, to do just as you please.' She sighed as she moved to the edge of the bed before standing up. 'Very well, Hawksmere. Arrange to take me to your torturers now and let us put an end to this.'

Looking at her from between narrowed lids, Zachary could not help but feel a certain grudging admiration for the calmness of Georgianna Lancaster's demeanour and the slender dignity of her stance. A dignity so at odds with the frivolously young and plumply desirable Georgianna Lancaster of just ten short months ago.

Zachary had not been consciously looking for his future wife the evening he attended the Duchess of St Albans' ball, only making that brief appearance because the duchess had been a friend of his deceased mother. He had thought only to while away an hour or so out of politeness to that lady before making his excuses and departing for somewhere he could enjoy some more sensual entertainments.

Indeed, he had been about to do exactly that when Georgianna Lancaster had chanced to dance by in the arms of some young rake. Even then it had been her eyes which first drew his attention.

Eyes whose colour Zachary had never seen before. Long-lashed and violet-coloured eyes, laughing up merrily into the face of the gentleman twirling her about the ballroom.

It had taken several more minutes for Zachary's hooded gaze to move lower, for his body to respond, to harden, at sight of those delectably pouting and sensual lips, the swell of full and creamy breasts above her gown and curvaceous, childbearing hips.

To say that his arousal at her abundance of femininity had come as something of a surprise to him was understating the matter.

Normally he did not so much as glance at any of the young débutantes paraded into society every Season, having long ago decided they were all prattling flirts who sought only a titled and wealthy husband, none of them having so much as a sensible thought in their giddy heads.

Georgianna Lancaster did not look any less giddy than her peers, but at least his manhood had sprung to attention at sight of her, a necessary function if one was in need of an heir, and, he had decided, the daughter of the Earl of Malvern would do as the mother of that heir as well as any.

He had even convinced himself that her youth was an asset rather than the burden an older, more demanding woman might become. He would be able to mould Georgianna to his ways; he could wed her and bed her, enjoy that lusciously ripe body to the full whilst he impregnated her, before then leaving her to enjoy her role as the Duchess of Hawksmere, and so allowing him to return to the more sophisticated entertainments he preferred.

Or so Zachary had decided as he had looked upon Georgianna Lancaster that evening ten months ago.

What he had not considered at the time, or for some days after the announcement of their betrothal appeared in the newspapers, was that Georgianna Lancaster had not been the one to accept his offer of marriage. That, young as she was, she had a mind of her own. She had no intention of becoming the wife of a man, even a duke, she neither knew nor loved.

Or so she'd stated in the letter she had left behind for her father to read after she had eloped with her French lover, and which Malvern had reluctantly shared with Zachary when he had demanded the older man do so.

Zachary's mouth thinned as he remembered the days following Georgianna's elopement with her French lover.

The formal withdrawal of the betrothal in the newspapers so soon after it had been announced.

The condolences he had received from his uncles and aunts.

Most humiliating of all, perhaps, had been the knowing looks of the *ton*, all of them aware that Zachary Black, the haughty Duke of Hawksmere, having finally chosen his future duchess, had then just days later been forced to retract the announcement when that future bride had withdrawn from the betrothal.

Or so the story had been related to society at large. Very few people were made privy to the knowledge of Georgianna's elopement with the young and handsome French tutor.

Certainly none knew that it had been discovered, after the elopement, that the French tutor was not who he'd claimed to be, but was in fact a spy.

As Georgianna Lancaster was herself now also a spy, at the behest of her French lover?

She certainly knew far too much of Zachary's private business, of his connections, to be the complete innocent she claimed to be.

'Your Grace?'

Zachary's eyes narrowed as he returned his attention to the here and now. 'If only it were as simple as that, Georgianna,' he bit out scathingly. 'Unfortunately, there are several aspects of your story which the two of us will need to discuss in more detail.'

'Such as?'

'Such as why you chose to come to me, of all people, with this fantastical tale.'

'It is not fantastical or a tale.'

'Why me, Georgianna?' he persisted.

Her lashes lowered over violet eyes. 'I—I can see no harm in my admitting that it was André who informed me that you had long been acting as a spy for the Crown.'

Zachary gave a humourless smile to cover the inner jolt her words had given him; if Rousseau knew of the work he carried out in secret for England, then surely it followed that others must also? 'Could you not have found more stimulating pillow talk?' he said scornfully.

Georgianna's cheeks coloured at the insult even as she straightened the narrowness of her shoulders determinedly. 'He taunted me with the knowledge when he…when he…'

'Yes?'

She raised her pointed little chin. 'When he admitted that he had never been in love with me.' Her lashes lowered, her voice husky. 'When he told me that he had deliberately seduced me, then used our elopement as a way of leaving England. That there were now some who suspected his real reason for being in England.'

Zachary nodded abruptly. 'He had only just been put under more intense investigation at the time of your elopement.' And if Rousseau now knew of Zachary's own secret work for the Crown, then his usefulness in that capacity had surely come to an end?

'How disappointing for you,' he drawled dismissively in order to cover his inner disquiet.

Violet eyes flashed rebelliously. 'Do not dare to mock me, your Grace.'

All humour faded as Zachary's mouth thinned in displeasure. 'Your behaviour these past ten months dictates that I shall now dare to treat you in whatever manner I please, madam.'

The fight went out of Georgianna as quickly as it had flared to life. She bowed her head, totally shamed at the truth of the duke's words. She had behaved like a fool ten months ago. A stupid and naïve fool who had fallen completely for André's charm.

A charm that had completely deserted him the night he had taunted her, mocked her, for having run away with him, a spy for Napoleon. When the man to whom she was betrothed, the man she had run away from, was in fact the honourable one and more of a hero to England than any but a select few knew.

'That still does not explain how you knew where I should be this evening.'

Georgianna raised her head wearily, too tired now to do any more than answer Zachary Black's questions. 'I returned to England by ship yesterday.'

'Does your brother know you are returned?' he prompted sharply.

'No one but you knows.' She gave a sad shake of her head. 'It would have been most unfair to burden Jeffrey with that knowledge.' Much as she might long to see her brother again, to know if he at least was able to forgive her for her past recklessness, he was still but nineteen years of age, and newly become the Earl of Malvern, with all of the responsibilities that title entailed. He did not need to be burdened with the knowledge of the return to England of his disgraced sister, too.

'Obviously you did not feel a need to treat me with the same consideration,' Hawksmere rasped disdainfully.

She winced. 'I have explained why you are different. Why I had no choice but to seek you out and speak with you.'

'But not how you knew where I should be this evening,' he reminded grimly.

'I made it my business to keep a watch of your comings and goings as soon as I arrived in London yesterday, in an effort to speak with you alone. This evening, spent at your club, to celebrate the nuptials of your friend, offered me the opportunity I needed.'

Hawksmere gave a dismissive shake of his head. 'I should have known if you had been following me.'

'Obviously you did not.'

Which was worrisome, Zachary acknowledged with a frown. It implied a complacency on his part now they were no longer at war, a laziness, if he had failed to realise he was being so closely watched.

He straightened. 'This has all been very interesting, I am sure, but I have several other things that require my attention this morning, not to forget a wedding to attend this afternoon. So I am afraid I cannot waste any more time on this particular conversation just now.'

She nodded. 'I am staying at lodgings in Duke Street—perhaps you can send word to me there once you are have decided what to do?'

'Oh, no, Georgianna, I am afraid that will not do at all,' Zachary drawled drily, grateful for the approximate knowledge of where she was staying in London. And that no one but he was aware of her presence back in England.

She stilled warily. 'What do you mean?'

'I mean that, for the moment, I cannot allow you to leave this bedchamber.'

She gasped. 'You cannot keep me a prisoner here.'

He eyed her mockingly. 'Can I not?'

'No.'

'And, pray tell, who is to stop me?'

Her hands clenched at her sides. 'You are attempting to frighten me again.'

'And succeeding?' Zachary prompted mildly.

'Not in the least.' Georgianna clamped her lips stubbornly together as she refused to show any fear at Hawksmere's threats.

As she refused to ever show fear again, of anything, or anyone, after the way she had suffered at Rousseau's hands.

Which did not mean that Georgianna was not inwardly quaking at the icy determination so clearly shown in Hawksmere's expression.

She repressed a shiver at how, just ten months ago, she had so narrowly escaped becoming the wife of this cold and ruthless gentleman. A man, Georgianna had no doubt, who would have settled her in one of his ducal homes following the wedding and then repeatedly bedded her, until she had filled his nursery with his heir and his spare. After which, like many of the gentlemen of the *ton*, he would no doubt have abandoned her to find her own entertainments, whilst he returned to the life he had enjoyed before their marriage.

Such, Georgianna knew, was the life of many wives in society. A loveless and boring existence.

A life she had hoped to escape when she had eloped with André.

Only to then find she had placed herself in an even more dire position than becoming Hawksmere's unloved duchess.

Did she regret her elopement of ten months ago?

Of course she did.

If she could live that time over again, she would have remained in England with her family.

And become the wife of Zachary Black, the Duke of Hawksmere instead?

Never!

Despite all that Georgianna had endured these past months, despite all that she might still have to endure, she did not have a single regret in regards to refusing to become the wife of the Duke of Hawksmere.

She would never marry at all now, of course. How could she, when her reputation was now such that no gentleman would ever consider making her his wife? And to lie about her past, to pose as a widow, perhaps, in order to marry a lower-born gentleman, was a deceit she refused to practise on any man, or any children born into that marriage.

No, Georgianna had accepted that she would spend the rest of her life alone. As she fully deserved to do, when her impetuous actions of ten months ago had resulted in such shame and scandal.

'Do not look so sad, Georgianna.' The duke deliberately chose to misunderstand the reason for that sadness as he crossed the bedchamber on predatory soft steps, until he now stood just inches away from her. 'I may be busy for the rest of the day, but I shall return later this evening. And when I do—' those glittering silver eyes held her mesmerised as he slowly raised a hand and allowed the hardness of his knuckles to graze softly over the warmth of her cheek '—I am sure we shall be able to think of several ways in which to keep you entertained, during your incarceration in my bedchamber.'

Georgianna gasped as she heard the intent beneath that softly sensuous voice. Just as she now flinched as the hardness of those knuckles travelled the length of her throat before moving lower, lingering to caress the swell of her breasts through the material of her gown.

Leaving her in absolutely no doubt as to what those entertainments might be.

Her cheeks burned with humiliated colour as she pulled back from those caressing knuckles. 'I may have fallen from decency in society's eyes, Hawksmere, but I assure you I have absolutely no intention of becoming your plaything.'

The duke eyed her derisively. 'The arousal of your breasts, from just the merest touch of my knuckles, tells a different story,' he drawled mockingly as he glanced pointedly downwards.

Georgianna's startled gaze followed the direction of his mocking gaze, her face paling as she saw what Hawksmere so obviously saw; those rosy berries that tipped her breasts were now swollen and full, and could clearly be seen outlined against the soft material of her gown buttoned up to her throat.

Because they were aroused?

By Hawksmere?

Impossible.

Oh, he was handsome enough to set any woman's heart beating faster. But it was a dangerous attraction, a challenge those silver eyes proclaimed no one woman would ever be able to satisfy.

Too much of a challenge, it was rumoured, for any woman, high- or low-born, married or unmarried, to resist sharing the duke's bed once he had expressed an interest.

But Georgianna was not one of those weak and susceptible women. How could she be, when she found Hawksmere no less intimidating now than she had ten months ago?

Except…

There was no denying the physical evidence of her breasts having become aroused by his lightest of touches.

Not with desire but fear, Georgianna instantly assured herself.

Because Hawksmere had just threatened to keep her here, a prisoner in his bedchamber, for as long as he chose to do so.

She straightened her spine. 'You cannot keep me here against my will,' she repeated firmly.

'I can do anything I wish with you, Georgianna,' Zachary murmured with satisfaction, mocking her response, her undeniable arousal at his caress.

An arousal which Zachary knew no woman could fabricate or control.

As he had been unable to control his own arousal

as he had lightly caressed the engorged tip of her breast.

Despite her having run away from marrying him ten months ago, Zachary could not deny that he still physically desired this woman. In his bed, beneath him, to be buried to the hilt between her thighs.

Try as he might, Zachary had found no explanation for that sudden clench of desire when he had looked at Georgianna Lancaster ten months ago, and he had none now, either. It was enough to know that it still existed.

A weakness, in the current circumstances, best kept to himself.

He stepped back abruptly. 'As I said, I have other things to occupy me this morning, but I will go downstairs now and arrange a breakfast for you, and then I advise that you get some sleep.'

'I am not hungry, nor shall I sleep.'

Zachary's eyes narrowed on her critically, noting the hollows in the paleness of her cheeks, her slenderness beneath the unbecoming black gown. 'You are grown too slender.'

'I said I am not hungry.' Those violet-coloured eyes flashed again in warning.

Another show of temper Zachary did not care for in the least, as he stepped deliberately closer to her, so close that he could see the way the pupils of her eyes expanded as she now looked up at him apprehensively.

'Nevertheless, you will eat all of the breakfast I have brought up to you.'

She maintained her ground even as a nerve pulsed rapidly at her throat, no doubt as evidence of her inner nervousness. 'And I have said I shall not.'

Once again Zachary felt that grudging admiration for her stubbornness; not too many people dared to stand against him, least of all women. She was a very young woman at that, and one who did not as yet appear to fully appreciate the danger she had placed herself in by choosing to step back into his life.

He gave a slow and deliberate smile. 'I advise you not to defy me, Georgianna.'

She eyed him rebelliously. 'Why should I not?'

He gave a nonchalant shrug as he murmured softly, 'Because I shall win and you will lose.'

Georgianna repressed another shiver of apprehension as she heard the arrogant certainty in his voice. As she acknowledged that, through her own stupidity this time, Hawksmere now had her completely at his mercy. She was his prisoner, to do with as he wished.

Hawksmere smiled confidently as he seemed to guess at least some of her thoughts. 'I shall be locking you in here in my absence, of course, and taking the key with me. And I advise that you not bother giving yourself a sore throat, or knuckles, by screaming or shouting, or banging on the door for my servants to release you whilst I am gone,' he added derisively. 'I shall make sure to inform them, before I depart, that it is all part of the erotic play between the two of us, and that the more you ask to be set free the more you desire to stay here and await my return.'

'You truly are a monster.' Georgianna's cheeks burned with humiliated colour.

He shrugged. 'I have never made any pretence of being anything else.'

The implication being, Georgianna knew, that she was the one who had practised deceit, when she'd lied to her family and her betrothed in order to run away with André.

And that Hawksmere believed she was lying to him even now.

Except she was not. And Hawksmere's decision to keep her locked up here, and his threats, did not change the fact that time was more the enemy than this arrogant duke. 'You will speak to someone this morning on my behalf?'

Hawksmere's mouth thinned into an uncompromising line. 'I have no plans to do so until the two of us have spoken again, no.'

'But you must,' Georgianna gasped desperately. 'Napoleon...'

'Enough, Georgianna,' Hawksmere rasped his impatience with her persistence as he grasped her arms, his silver eyes as cold as ice as he looked down the length of his arrogant nose at her. 'I have not had the opportunity to sleep, either, this past night, and my patience is now at an end.'

'But...'

'I said enough, Georgianna,' he thundered.

Tears blurred her vision. 'You have every right to be angry with me, to despise me for my having ended our betrothal in the way that I did.' She gave a weary shake of her head. 'Take your revenge upon me any way you please. I do not care what you do to me, as long as you take my warnings seriously.'

'And if it is my wish to claim your body, for your having run from me, from our betrothal, ten months ago?' he taunted softly.

She shook her head. 'As long as you also listen to me in regards to Napoleon.'

'One more mention of that man's name and more pressing responsibilities be damned, I shall be forced to begin that punishment now!' the duke warned darkly. 'Now that I think about it, it might be best if I were to request that you remove your gown,' he mused hardly. 'You will be less likely to attempt an escape if you are half-naked.'

'I will not take off my gown.' Georgianna pulled out of his grasp to move quickly away from him, her hands held up defensively in front of her rapidly rising and falling chest.

Zachary studied her through narrowed lids as he noted the wild panic in those beautiful violet-coloured eyes. Much like a deer the moment it realised it was caught in the sights of the hunter's gun.

All because he had asked her to remove her gown?

Surely a woman who had shared one man's bed for the past ten months would not be quite so averse to the idea of another man seeing her naked?

Unless…

'Did he hurt you?' Zachary scowled darkly.

That violet gaze sharpened. 'What?'

His mouth thinned. 'Did Rousseau hurt you?'

'Of course he hurt me! How could he not, when he used me to make good his escape?'

'That is not the type of hurt I am referring to, Georgianna.' Zachary took several steps towards her, coming to a halt as Georgianna shadowed those steps by moving back, until she was now pressed up against one of the velvet curtains hanging at the window. 'I have no intentions of harming you, Georgianna.'

She gave a choked and bitter laugh. 'You have just threatened to take away my gown.'

'And that is all I have threatened.'

She gave a shudder. 'It is enough!'

Zachary's eyes narrowed. 'Some men like to give pain to their bed partner during lovemaking, as a way of heightening their own arousal.'

She gasped. 'Do you?' Pale and slender fingers now tightly clasped at the throat of that unbecoming black gown as she stared at him with dark and shadowed eyes.

'No, I most certainly do not,' Zachary assured grimly. 'But I am beginning to suspect that Rousseau did. Do you perhaps share his perversion?'

'No!'

'I am glad to hear it.' Zachary's eyes narrowed. 'But has he left lasting marks upon your body you would not wish another man to see?' he added harshly, surprised at how violent it made him feel to think of there being so much as a single bruise administered to that alabaster skin, let alone any lasting reminder of the man Rousseau.

Georgianna breathed shallowly, not sure she understood all that Zachary Black was saying to her. Not sure she wanted to understand.

Surely lovemaking was exactly that? An expression of the love a couple felt for one another? Or if not love, then at least a tenderness, a caring, for the other's welfare?

What the duke was describing, the deliberate inflicting of pain, did not sound as if it could be any of those things.

And yet Georgianna did indeed bear scars, and ones inflicted upon her by André Rousseau. Not the visible scars to which Hawksmere seemed to refer, of course, but they were damning none the less. A testament to the scorn, the total uninterest in which André had held the impressionable young girl who had forsaken all for her love of him.

'I can see that he did.' Hawksmere obviously took her silence to be her answer, his expression grimmer than ever. 'And you still love such a man?' he added disgustedly.

'No.' Georgianna choked in protest; how could she possibly love a man who had treated her as André had?

To her everlasting shame, Georgianna was no longer sure she had ever really loved André, or whether she had not just been in love with love itself.

A year ago she had been so young and idealistic, had believed in love and romance. And the handsome and penniless Frenchman employed by her father had seemed so much more romantic, so much easier to love than the intimidating and distant Duke of Hawksmere. To the extent that Georgianna had woven all of her dreams about the golden-haired and romantic Frenchman in order to run away from marrying the dangerous duke.

Reality had proven to be so much less than those silly, romantic dreams.

Not that she believed Hawksmere to be any less dangerous now than she had previously. The opposite, after the things he had said and done to her today.

But she certainly had no romantic dreams left in regard to André Rousseau, either, or indeed any other man.

Hawksmere's top lip curled up in distaste, silver eyes a pale glitter between narrowed lids. 'Again, this is something we will have to discuss further upon my return. No doubt we shall have the opportunity to discuss many things during the hours we spend here in my bedchamber together,' he added pleasantly.

'How long do you intend to keep me here?' Georgianna stared at him disbelievingly.

'As long as it takes to get to the truth,' Zachary assured uninterestedly.

She gave a desperate shake of her head. 'Have you not listened to a word I have said? Do you not understand the urgency of the things I have told you?'

He eyed her mockingly. 'I have listened to the little you decided to share with me, yes.'

'What will it take to convince you of my sincerity?'

'More than you have already told me, obviously,' Zachary drawled drily, brows raised questioningly.

A frown creased Georgianna's forehead as she obviously fought an inner battle as to how much more she intended revealing to him.

Finally she gave a defeated sigh. 'Napoleon is to leave Elba before the end of this month.'

'And you come to me with this story now?' He raised sceptical brows. 'With the end of the month just days away?'

'I did not—' Georgianna gave an impatient shake of her head as she accepted that to Hawksmere this was still just a 'story'. 'I only learnt of the plan nine days ago and I could not immediately get passage from France. I…' Her gaze lowered. 'André has men placed at all of the ports, watching and waiting for anyone who might wish to betray Napoleon.'

'And yet here you are,' Hawksmere drawled disbelievingly.

She nodded. 'But I had to bide my time and make good my escape when the chance came for me to join a large family travelling together. I was all the time fearful that someone might recognise me. Am I boring you, your Grace?' she prompted sharply as the duke gave a yawn.

'As it happens, yes, you are.' He nodded unapologetically.

'But…'

'I really am uninterested in listening to any more buts or arguments just now, Georgianna,' he rasped harshly.

Georgianna looked up searchingly into his hard and implacable face. Noting the cold glitter of his silver eyes. The tautness of the skin across sculptured cheekbones. The sneering curl of his top lip.

The determined set of his arrogant and unyielding jaw.

She knew in that moment that all of her efforts of appeal for Zachary Black's help had been a waste of her time.

That this man despised her so utterly he would never believe a single word she said to him.

Chapter Four

Zachary was irritable and tired by the time he returned home several hours later, his morning having proved to be a frustrating one.

Not least because the man he had wished to speak with, the man to whom he had reported this past four years, was unavailable, and likely to be so for the next few days, as his deputy had informed Zachary. It happened, of course, but it was frustrating, nevertheless.

He had duly passed along the relevant information to the deputy, of course, but even so he still felt a sense of dissatisfaction.

It was true that there had been dozens of rumours of plots and plans to liberate the Corsican from Elba these past months and each and every one of them had necessarily to be investigated.

What if Georgianna were telling the truth and Napoleon really did mean to leave Elba before the month's end and return to the shores of France? Possibly as emperor? That would not suit Louis or England.

Zachary had also requested to look at the file they had accumulated on André Rousseau these past months, hoping it might shed some light upon Georgianna Lancaster's own movement. There had been no sightings of her in Rousseau's company for some months. No sightings of her at all, it seemed, since a week or so after she and Rousseau had arrived in Paris together.

A curiosity in itself.

Where had Georgianna been all this time? And what had she been doing? For that matter, if she had not been with Rousseau, then where had she come by the information regarding Napoleon?

For the moment Zachary's instructions were clear; he was to continue to keep Georgianna Lancaster imprisoned in his home and continue questioning her until such time as he was notified otherwise.

For all that Zachary had earlier today taunted Georgianna with the possibility of her continued incarceration, he was not best pleased at receiving orders to do exactly that.

And one of the main reasons for that was Georgianna herself.

The previous year she had been an inexperienced and idealistic young girl, that plump and desirable pigeon that Zachary had decided to marry, bed and subsequently mould into being his undemanding duchess.

Just a few minutes in her company earlier this morning and Zachary knew that Georgianna's ten months in France had wrought more changes in her than just the physical ones.

That bright-eyed young girl, eager for life, was no more. And in her place was a coolly dignified, capable and stubborn woman. One who had lived in Paris, by all accounts, completely alone for some months, before arranging her own passage back to England. Who had then managed to follow him without his knowledge, until such time as she was able to speak with him privately. Moreover, Georgianna had shown him that very morning she was not a woman who intended to ever be cowed, by him, or anyone else.

If anything, that air of dignity, her independence and intelligence, appealed to and aroused Zachary even more than that naïve young woman he had intended to make his wife.

And whatever else Georgianna might claim to be now, she had eloped with André Rousseau ten months ago. She had been the Frenchman's lover for a number of weeks, if not months, before and following that elopement.

For Zachary to feel desire and admiration for such a woman, a woman he had every reason to distrust, was not only rash on his part, but it could also be dangerous.

Zachary drew in a deep breath as he came to a halt outside the door to his bedchamber, noting there was no sound coming from within. He had questioned his butler on his arrival, and been informed that all had been silent above stairs all morning. Georgianna had obviously taken Zachary's advice to heart and refrained from screaming, or banging on the door, demanding to be set free.

And perhaps that had just been a ploy and she was even now poised behind the silence of that door, candelabrum in hand, ready to knock Zachary senseless before making good her escape?

His smile was grim as he quietly unlocked the door to his bedchamber. He entered softly and saw the room was in semi-darkness, the curtains pulled halfway across the two picture windows, nevertheless allowing him to see that the breakfast tray still sat on the table near the door where he had placed it earlier.

The untouched breakfast tray.

A single glance was enough to show him that none of the food on the plates had been eaten. Only the dregs left in the bottom of the delicate china cup to show that Georgianna had drunk her tea at least.

The half-drawn curtains allowed the weak February sunshine to shaft across the room to where Georgianna lay asleep on top of his bed. She was still dressed in that unbecoming black gown. The curling ebony hair had been loosened, however, and now flowed thick and silky over the pillows behind her and across her breasts down to her tiny waist.

Zachary put down the bag he carried to cross softly to the bedside and look down at her. Her face appeared as a beautiful pale oval in the weak light. Long lashes fanned silkily against ivory cheeks as she continued to sleep, her rosy and sensual lips slightly parted as she breathed softly and evenly.

A deceptive picture of innocence, if not beauty.

So she might once have looked in their marriage bed, Zachary acknowledged with annoyance as his traitorous body stirred, hardened, as he continued to look down at her. And he had no doubt that until a year ago she had been an innocent, those violet-coloured eyes full of joy, of the expectations of life, rather than swirling with dark shadows as they had been earlier today.

Feeling any sort of empathy, sympathy, for this woman would be a mistake on his part. Most especially when he still questioned her real motives for seeking him out.

Zachary's mouth thinned as he turned away impatiently and walked determinedly from the bedside with the intention of pulling the curtains completely across the windows. He had no time to rest himself— he had Wilding's wedding to attend—but Georgianna might as well continue to sleep peacefully.

Zachary was in need of a bath and a change of clothes after his own sleepless night, before he then attended the wedding in just a few hours.

'Leave them. Please.'

Zachary gave a start at the sound of Georgianna's voice. A voice that sounded as if it were underlined with panic. Or possibly fear? Simply because he had been about to draw the last of the curtains fully across the windows to shut out the daylight?

He turned to see that Georgianna had moved up on to her elbows, those ebony curls falling past her shoulders and cascading back on to the pillows behind her.

Her face was still that ghostly oval, her eyes so

dark they appeared almost purple as she looked across at him pleadingly. 'Please,' she beseeched earnestly.

'What is it, Georgianna?' Zachary prompted sharply as he crossed, frowning, to her side.

Her breasts quickly rose and fell. 'I—I am afraid of… I do not like complete dark.' She sat up abruptly to curl her arms defensively about her drawn-up knees, looking for all the world like that frightened deer of earlier.

'What foolishness is this, Georgianna?' Zachary chided impatiently. 'If you think to appeal to my softer side with exhibitions of feminine—'

'How could I possibly do that, when we both know you do not have a softer side for me to appeal to!' she came back sharply as she moved swiftly to the side of the bed before standing up and crossing to the window on stockinged feet. There she pulled back the curtains to allow in the full daylight. 'And I assure you I speak only the truth.' Her hands, no longer hidden in those black lace gloves, were clasped tightly together in front of her, the knuckles white as she looked up at him. 'I do not like to be in the complete dark. Ever.' Her lips firmed as she raised her chin in challenge.

Zachary ignored Georgianna's insult as he continued to study her through narrowed lids. Her face was ashen, but that could be because she had not slept for long enough, nor had she eaten the breakfast he had had brought to her.

No, it was those tightly clasped hands, and the defiance in her stance, which now convinced Zachary that she was sincere in her dislike, even fear, of the complete dark.

'And why is that?' he prompted softly.

Georgianna swallowed, hating that she had shown any sign of weakness in front of Zachary Black, the mocking Duke of Hawksmere. She hated him for dwelling on that weakness, whereas before she had merely feared him.

Nor did she have any intention of telling this hateful man of the head injury she had suffered and which, for two weeks, had left her blind. For that short time she had been caught in eternal darkness, afraid that she would never be able to see again.

It had been fear unlike anything Georgianna had ever known before, including the bleakness of those hours after André had attempted to murder her, leaving her body in the woods for the wild animals to devour.

She accepted she had wronged Zachary Black in the past and had apologised for it, but surely, surely she did not have to now reveal all of her humiliations so that he might taunt her further?

She hoped to keep some dignity.

'How did you get that?' she demanded sharply, eyes wide as she saw and recognised her travelling bag sitting on the floor just inside the door of the bedchamber.

Hawksmere gave it a cursory glance before turning back with a dismissive shrug. 'It was collected from your lodgings this morning, of course.'

'I— But— How did you know where…? I told you

earlier the name of the street where I had taken lodgings,' Georgianna confirmed heavily.

'You did, yes.' Zachary gave a hard smile of satisfaction. It had not taken long at all for one of his footmen to be sent to Duke Street to discover in which lodging Georgianna was staying. 'It was not too difficult to guess that the Anna Smith, who arrived in London yesterday, was in fact Georgianna Lancaster,' he added coolly as she seemed to have been struck momentarily dumb. 'And the two small portraits on the dressing table of your mother and father together, and another of your brother, confirmed it was so.'

Those violet eyes rose quickly to meet his. 'You went to Mrs Jenkins's house yourself?'

He shrugged. 'I did not think you would appreciate having one of my footmen pawing through your more personal items.'

She bristled. 'Obviously you did not hesitate to do so yourself.'

'Obviously not.' Zachary gave a mocking nod. 'We may have fought a war with France, but I have always considered that they do make the most sensual of ladies' undergarments.'

Two spots of colour appeared in the paleness of Georgianna's cheeks. 'And no doubt you have seen enough of them to be an expert on the subject?'

'No doubt.' Zachary's mouth quirked in amusement. 'Is it not a little late for you to be exhibiting such maidenly outrage, Georgianna?' he added hardly.

He was right. Of course he was right, Georgianna

acknowledged heavily. She knew she had forfeited any right to feel outrage, maidenly or otherwise, in Hawksmere's eyes, as well as those of all decent society, the moment she left her home in the middle of the night and eloped with André.

Except, unbelievable as it would undoubtedly be for others to learn, she was still a maiden…

She and André had spent the first night and day of their elopement travelling by coach to the port where they intended to board the boat bound for France, their intention being to marry there rather than linger overlong in England. And André had explained, once they reached that port, that they stood more chance of remaining undetected if they travelled as brother as sister. A logic for which Georgianna had been exceedingly grateful.

Not least because, by that time, she had begun to doubt the wisdom of her actions.

It had all seemed so romantic, so exciting, when she and André made their plans to elope together in the middle of the night. But the long hours spent in the coach together, the rattling and jostling too severe to allow sleep or even rest, and fraying both their tempers and patience, had enabled Georgianna to see André as rather less than the romantic hero she had thought him to be.

To realise that, by running away with André in the middle of the night, she had cut herself off completely from her family, from society, in a scandal so shocking she would never be able to return.

The respite of travelling on the boat together as

brother and sister had been something of a balm to her already frayed nerves.

To accept that she was no longer as sure that she wished to become André's wife at all.

Considering the nightmare that had followed, it was perhaps as well she had already begun to have those doubts.

She drew herself up to her full height of just over five feet as she now met Hawksmere's gaze unflinchingly. 'I trust you are not expecting me to thank you for something that was unnecessary in the first place?'

'Oh, it was very necessary, Georgianna,' he corrected harshly. 'As I informed you earlier, you are to remain here for the next few days. And I thought you might feel more comfortable if you had your own things with you.'

Georgianna's head ached from having awoken so suddenly, in response to Hawksmere shutting out the daylight. The same response, panic and fear, she always felt now at finding herself in complete darkness.

Nevertheless, headache or no, she could not allow Hawksmere's words to go unchallenged. 'We both know your only concern was to allay Mrs Jenkins's suspicions when I did not return there later today. No doubt she was suitably impressed at the presence of the illustrious Duke of Hawksmere in her modest home?'

He gave that derisive smile. 'No doubt.'

Georgianna gave a disgusted shake of her head.

'You really do mean to keep me a prisoner here, then?'

His jaw tightened. 'For the moment, yes.'

She sighed. 'An occurrence which I can see does not suit you any more than it does me.'

He shrugged his wide shoulders. 'It would seem that neither one of us has a choice in the matter. But there is a bright side to all of this, Georgianna,' he added softly as he crossed the bedchamber with those soft and predatory steps. 'Just think, you did not have to marry me in order to share my bedchamber.'

Georgianna refused to be intimidated as Hawksmere now stood just inches away from her. So close, in fact, that she could see every detail of the livid scar upon his throat, as well as the dark stubble on his jaw, evidence that he had not yet had time to shave today. Indeed, his evening clothes from the night before showed that he had not so much as taken the time to change his clothes yet this morning.

Because, despite his scepticism towards her earlier, he had believed enough of what she told him to not waste any time in sharing that information?

Georgianna certainly hoped that was the case.

She could bear any amount of Hawksmere's mockery, as well as his scorn and disgust, if at the same time he helped to thwart this latest plot to liberate Napoleon from Elba.

She gave a humourless smile. 'We must all be grateful for small mercies, your Grace.'

Zachary's bark of laughter was completely spontaneous. A genuine appreciation of Georgianna's continued feistiness, despite the direness of the situation in which she now found herself.

And not much succeeded in amusing Zachary any more.

As an only child, he had inherited the Hawksmere title eleven years ago, upon the death of both his parents in a carriage accident. The years that followed had been lonely as well as busy ones, mainly filled with the responsibilities of his title, and fighting against Napoleon, in open battle, and secretly as an agent for the Crown.

Those same years had shown him that women, young and old, thin or plump, fair or dark, single or married, were willing to do almost anything for the attentions of a duke. This had resulted in a jading, a cynicism within him, beyond Zachary's control.

It appeared Georgianna Lancaster was the exception.

Not only had she chosen to run away from becoming his duchess ten months ago, but even now she continued to defy and challenge him in ways that no other woman ever had.

'I believe I prefer you feisty and defiant, Georgianna, rather than the naïve ninny you were ten months ago,' Zachary murmured appreciatively as he looked down searchingly into the pale face she held up to challenge him. The arching of her slender neck allowed those ebony curls to fall silkily down the length of her spine to her pert little bottom.

'A naïve ninny you nevertheless intended to make your wife,' she reminded scathingly.

He shrugged. 'I believed you to be a malleable ninny then.'

Her brows rose. 'And now?'

Zachary gave a slow and appreciative smile. 'Now I believe this added fire makes you more appealing than I might otherwise have expected.'

Georgianna shuddered, keeping a watchful eye on Hawksmere as she instinctively took a step back from him. She was wary of the way in which his eyes now glittered down at her so intently, almost as if a white light had been ignited in those silver depths. Georgianna was unsure of precisely what that flame might mean, but she did know that she no longer wished to stand quite so close to him.

Hawksmere took that same step forward before raising his hand to gently cup one side of her face, the soft pad of his thumb moving in a soft caress across her parted lips. 'There is nowhere you would be able to run this time, Georgianna, that I would not find you.'

Her heart was beating rapidly in her chest: at Hawksmere's threats, his proximity, and the effects of that caressing thumb against her lips. A sensuous caress, much as Georgianna might wish it otherwise, which caused a heat to course through her whole body, leaving her skin feeling flushed and tight and her breasts swelling uncomfortably beneath her gown.

Because, as Hawksmere had claimed earlier, she was aroused by his touch?

How could that possibly be, when she disliked this

man, when she had run from him, from the very idea of becoming his wife, less than a year ago?

Perhaps it was just that she had been alone, and lonely, for so very long? Too long without the gentle touch of another? Since she had been held by another? Looked at with warmth, if not affection?

Except the warmth in Hawksmere's gaze was so clearly predatory rather than affectionate.

Georgianna pulled back sharply from the mesmerising effect of that silver gaze. 'I have no intentions of running anywhere,' she assured him decisively. At least, not until this matter of Napoleon's liberation was settled. 'Did you go to your superior this morning and report my information?'

Zachary continued to look down at Georgianna for several long moments more. His response to her was undeniable. To her beauty, her proximity, to having touched and caressed those soft and pouting lips. Totally undeniable, when his erection pressed so insistently against the front of his breeches.

'And what business is it of yours whether I did or I did not?' He arched a challenging brow.

'But…' she blinked her bewilderment '…I am the one responsible for giving you that information.'

He nodded abruptly. 'All the more reason for it to be mistrusted, surely? What did you expect, Georgianna?' he taunted as she looked pained. 'Did you think that by returning to England, by twittering about some ridiculous plot of how Napoleon intends to leave Elba before the end of the month, that all would be forgiven? That you would be a heroine, and could then return to your family, to society?' he prompted cruelly.

Those striking eyes became misty with unshed tears. 'I am well aware there can be no forgiveness, in any quarter, for the way I have behaved,' she spoke so softly Zachary could barely hear her, as her tears fell unchecked down the paleness of her cheeks.

Zachary felt instant regret for his deliberate cruelty. Whatever this woman might have done to him personally in the past, there was an undeniable vulnerability about her now, an aloneness, that Zachary knew he could relate to.

He breathed deeply through his nose. 'Perhaps that situation is not quite so bleak as you think it is.'

She tilted her head curiously. 'What do you mean?'

He owed this woman nothing except his contempt and distrust, Zachary reminded himself impatiently. Certainly not absolution for her deeds of ten months ago.

And yet…

He was not a deliberately cruel man, no matter what others might say or think to the contrary. He considered their past association.

Could Georgianna really be blamed for what had happened in their past? She was a young girl of only nineteen who'd feared, to the extent of running away from marriage to a man who had not even troubled himself in getting to know her before offering for her. He'd been a man who had not even spoken to her before making that offer. And once made, she'd had that offer accepted by her father without knowing a thing about it—or him.

Much as it galled him, Zachary knew he must accept some of the blame for the way in which Georgianna had run away back then.

But not for what had happened since that time, or the possible depth of her continued involvement with Rousscau.

He hardened his heart against the idea of telling Georgianna of the way in which he and her father had, between them, managed to salvage her reputation at least, if not their own embarrassment.

'A place can always be found in a gentleman's life for a beautiful woman,' he rasped insultingly.

Her throat moved as she swallowed. 'As his mistress, you mean?'

Zachary bared his teeth in a humourless smile. 'But of course.'

'I believe I should rather become an old maid,' she answered with quiet dignity.

'Do not make your decision based on your experience with Rousseau, Georgianna,' he advised coldly. 'Being the mistress of a gentleman would not be like it was with him. You would have a house of your own. Servants. An elegant carriage. A generous allowance, for clothing and such.'

Her chin rose. 'You, of course, would know of such things.'

In actual fact, Zachary had no personal knowledge of such an arrangement. He had never been enamoured enough of any of the women he had bedded in the past to have so much as ever considered making any his permanent mistress.

What sort of mistress would Georgianna make? The depths to those violet-coloured eyes, the sensual pout of her lips, and the uncontrollable response of her breasts to his lightest touch, all spoke of a passionate nature. Of a woman who was more than capable of meeting his physical demands with an equal fire.

And that she was untrustworthy?

Perhaps that might even add to the excitement, the danger, of such an arrangement?

He was a fool for even considering taking Georgianna Lancaster as a mistress, when there was no question that she had been mistress to Rousseau. Might still be so, for all Zachary knew of that situation.

'Not recently, no,' he answered bitingly. 'Which means the position is currently available, if you are interested in applying?' He raised goading brows.

Georgianna drew herself up proudly. 'So that you might insult me by refusing, no doubt?'

'No doubt.'

She gave a shake of her head. 'I am not, nor will I ever be, interested in such a role, in your life or any other man's.'

Zachary gave a hard smile. 'It is the only one still available to you.'

'I said I am not interested,' she repeated firmly.

'Then I will see that the bedchamber adjoining this one is prepared for your use. Yes, I too appreciate the irony of having you now occupy the bedchamber intended for my duchess,' he drawled as Georgianna's eyes widened. 'But it would seem that for the moment, at least, I am to have little choice in the matter.'

'You have the choice of releasing me—you just refuse to take it,' Georgianna pointed out sharply.

'I do, yes.' The duke gave a haughty inclination of his head. 'But I do not intend to keep you prisoner all the time, Georgianna. When I return later this evening you will join me downstairs for dinner. And I wish you to wear the lilac gown I brought from your lodgings rather than the black.'

'I will not be told by you what I shall do or what I shall wear.'

'You will if you do not wish to find yourself face first over my knee, with your skirts thrown up to your waist, whilst I thrash your bare bottom a rosy red for daring to disobey!' Hawksmere assured harshly.

Georgianna gasped at the crudeness of the threat. A threat she knew this man to be more than capable of carrying out. 'You are a barbarian, sir.'

He bared his teeth in a smile. 'All men are barbarians at heart, my lady.'

Georgianna repressed a shudder as the conversation brought back the painful memory of the violence she had suffered at André's hands. A violence she would not have believed possible of the once gentle man she had thought she knew and loved. A violence which had left her both blind and fighting for her life.

Again she wondered if Hawksmere would believe her, trust that she only spoke the truth, if she were to tell him of that terrible night when André had tried to kill her. When he thought he had killed her. It was only luck, and the arrival of a local farmer who had heard the shots being fired and feared for his livestock, that had ensured she had not died that night.

'What are you thinking about?' Hawksmere demanded shrewdly.

Would he believe her if she were to show him the scars her body carried from that night?

They were undoubtedly the scars left by a bullet wound, but there was no guarantee, even if Georgianna were to bare her flesh, that Hawksmere would any more believe it was André Rousseau himself who had inflicted them than the duke believed the information she had brought to him regarding Bonaparte's intended escape from Elba.

Georgianna had little in her life now except the small amount of pride left to her. She feared she might lose that, too, if Hawksmere were to both ridicule and scorn, and to disbelieve the physical scars she bore as proof of André Rousseau's complete disregard for her.

Hatred was far too strong a word to use to describe the calculated way in which André had come to the conclusion that she had outlived her purpose. He had been completely unemotional that night in the woods before he shot her, having assured her it was not a personal action, rather it was that he had no more use for her.

She could not bear to now have Zachary Black, the scornful Duke of Hawksmere, prod and poke at the even deeper wound that had been inflicted that night upon her heart and soul.

She raised her chin. 'I do not care for your threats.'

'No?'

'No!'

He shrugged wide shoulders. 'Then do as I say and wear the lilac gown for dinner this evening.'

'I am not hungry.'

'You will eat, Georgianna,' Hawksmere bit out determinedly. 'As I also have to eat. And I have no intentions of looking across my dinner table at the unpleasant sight of a scarecrow in a black mourning gown.'

She drew in a sharp breath. 'You are exceedingly cruel.'

'I am, yes,' he acknowledged unapologetically. 'Perhaps if you had eaten your breakfast, as I instructed you to do...' He shrugged. 'But you did not, so there it is.'

'I told you then, I was not hungry.'

'And I distinctly recall telling you that you are too thin,' he countered forcefully. 'You look as if a stray breath of wind might blow you away. It is a fact that most gentlemen prefer a little meat on their women.'

'It is not my intention to be attractive to any gentleman.'

'Then you have succeeded. Admirably so, in fact,' Hawksmere added grimly.

'And most especially to you,' she concluded fiercely.

'Most especially me?' he repeated softly, dark brows raised speculatively.

'Yes.' Her cheeks were flushed.

Hawksmere gave a slow smile. 'Then I am sorry

to inform you that I do not appear to find the loss of your curves to have affected my own physical ardour in the slightest.'

'And I am sorry to inform you that I am not in the least interested in a single one of your likes or dislikes,' she replied heatedly.

'I believe you made that more than obvious when you broke our betrothal to elope with another man.'

Georgianna blinked at the harshness of his tone. As if he might actually have cared about her ten months ago?

But of course he had cared, she reminded herself heavily. Oh, not about her, but he most certainly cared about the blow she had dealt him by running away with André. But it was Hawksmere's pride which had been injured, not his heart. Because he had no heart to injure?

He drew in an impatient breath. 'I do not have the time to discuss this any further just now, Georgianna. I have a wedding to get to.' He eyed her irritably. 'If you were to stop being so damned difficult, then I might arrange for a bath to be brought up to you later this afternoon. You would like that, would you not?'

Georgianna had no interest in dining with this cold and insulting man, no interest in eating, nor being in Hawksmere's company any more than she had to be.

But if agreeing to wear the lilac gown, and sitting down to dinner with him this evening, also ensured she was allowed the luxury of a bath, then perhaps it would not be so bad? She might even find the chance to escape this house some time during the evening.

'You obviously know something of a woman's weaknesses, your Grace.'

He gave another of those humourless smiles. 'You have the honour of being one of the women from whom I have learnt that particular lesson, Georgianna.'

Her gaze dropped from meeting his at the obvious reference to her elopement with André. 'Very well, I will wear the lilac gown and sit down to dinner with you,' she conceded quietly. 'But I warn you again, I have little appetite.'

Her breath caught in her throat at the intensity of Hawksmere's gaze as he now crossed the distance between them on stealthy feet, her heart fluttering wildly in her chest as she refused to give ground when he came to a halt in front of her.

He smiled slightly at her defiance as he raised his hand and once again cupped the side of her face. He ran the soft pad of his thumb across the swell of her bottom lip. 'Not to worry, Georgianna, I believe I can find appetite enough for the both of us this evening,' he promised gruffly, his gaze continuing to hold hers for several long seconds, before he abruptly lowered his head to sweep the firmness of his lips across hers. 'So soft,' he murmured appreciatively, his breath warm as those lips now trailed caressingly across the paleness of her cheek to her earlobe, teeth gently biting.

Georgianna was too stunned by the unexpected intimacy to be able to move, could barely breathe, as her heart pounded erratically in her chest.

Hawksmere raised his head to look down at her for several long seconds, silver eyes glittering, before he straightened abruptly and turned on his heel to cross the room and depart, followed seconds later by the sound of the door locking behind him.

Leaving Georgianna in a state of complete emotional turmoil.

Chapter Five

'You see how much pleasanter it is when you do as I ask, Georgianna?' Zachary mocked several hours later as he pulled back a chair for her to sit down at the dinner table before taking his place in the chair beside her.

He had left instructions that he and Georgianna would be dining together in the smaller, more intimate dining room. A fire crackled merrily in the hearth, and two three-pronged candelabra illuminated the crystal glassware and silver cutlery. A bowl of pale pink roses had also been placed in the centre of the small round table.

To her credit, Georgianna had been ready and waiting for Zachary when he'd unlocked the door and entered the bedchamber adjoining his own, her expression one of cool composure as she stood in the middle of the room.

The darkness of her hair was smooth and shining and once again secured at her crown, with those tantalising bunches of curls at her temples and nape. The lilac gown had darkened her eyes to that deep violet. Her face was a pale ivory, her lips a full and rosy pout against that pallor.

Zachary shifted uncomfortably now as he realised he was once again aroused by the sight and scent of her.

No other woman had ever physically aroused him as easily as this one appeared to.

Zachary's gaze narrowed on her critically as she smiled her thanks up at Hinds as he poured wine into her glass. What was it about this woman in particular that she managed to hold him in a constant state of arousal?

She was undoubtedly a beautiful young woman, her hair so dark and silky, and her delicately lovely face dominated by those violet-coloured eyes. And the lilac gown was certainly an improvement on that unbecoming black. But even so the style of the new gown still left a lot to be desired. It was not particularly fashionable, with its high neckline buttoned all the way up to her throat, revealing none of the tempting swell of her breasts as so many other women did nowadays, some of them to a degree of indecency.

Zachary had seen, and bedded, many beautiful women in his lifetime and all had been more fashionable and some more beautiful than Georgianna. So why was it that she affected him in a physical way he appeared to have absolutely no control over?

He should not have kissed her earlier, of course. Certainly should not have enjoyed the softness of her lips quite so much as he had, to the point that he had almost said to hell with attending Worthing's wedding and carried Georgianna back to the bed instead. It was not a pleasant realisation for a man who had always put duty, and the well-being of his close friends, first.

'I should have worn the lilac gown this evening in any case.'

It took Zachary several moments to pull out of the bleakness of his thoughts and realise that Georgianna was now answering his own earlier comment. Defiantly. Challengingly.

And there he had it.

This was the way in which Georgianna differed to every other woman Zachary had ever met. Because no man, or woman, had ever dared to defy or challenge the will of the Duke of Hawksmere.

That plump pigeon of ten months ago had undoubtedly feared him, as much as she had feared becoming his wife, but this Georgianna gave the impression that she feared nothing and no one. Except…

'Have you always disliked being in complete dark?'

Georgianna had not been expecting the question. Although perhaps she should have done; Hawksmere was a man who liked to disarm his adversaries rather than put them at their ease. As he had just done by unexpectedly mentioning her fear of darkness.

As he had disarmed her a short time ago, when he had unlocked and entered her bedchamber through the door which adjoined that room to his own. Looking every inch the handsome and highly eligible Duke of Hawksmere, dressed in impeccably tailored black evening clothes and snowy-white linen, his fashionably overlong hair a damp and ebony sheen about that saturnine face. A face dominated by those piercing silver eyes.

As sitting beside him now at the dinner table, the warmth of his thigh almost touching her own, was also disarming her.

Only because he had unexpectedly kissed her earlier, she reassured herself impatiently. A totally unwelcome kiss.

A kiss she had nevertheless been unable to forget in the hours that followed.

Instead of the suppressed violence she might have expected, Hawksmere's kiss had been gentle, searching, as if seeking a response from her rather than demanding one.

And all these hours since Georgianna had questioned if in fact she had responded.

It had been such a fleeting kiss, a mere brushing of Hawksmere's lips against her own, and Georgianna had been so surprised by it that she had no memory of whether or not she had returned the pressure of those firm lips. She certainly hoped not, but still she could not be sure.

She turned to him with cool eyes. 'I have been wondering about that wound to your throat, and the possibility it was inflicted by another female who was equally as unwilling to become your duchess?'

And there he had it again, Zachary acknowledged,

as he began to smile and then to chuckle openly; not only did Georgianna challenge him, but she also had the ability to make him laugh, at himself as much as others. 'There have been no others females, unwilling or otherwise, whom I have asked to become my duchess.' He finally sobered enough to answer her.

'You surprise me.'

He gave a mocking inclination of his head. 'My only unsatisfactory venture into contemplating the married state has made me wary of repeating the experience.'

'Then your wound really was, as it is rumoured, inflicted by a French sabre?' She was barely able to suppress a shiver.

Zachary's humour faded, his expression darkening as he ran his fingertips along the six-inch length of the scar. It had been with him for so long now that he rarely thought about it any more. Or the effect it might have upon others. Upon Georgianna. 'You find it repulsive?'

'I find the idea of the violence behind it repulsive, yes,' she answered him carefully.

'Indeed?' he rasped.

'I did not mean you any insult,' Georgianna assured hastily. 'I—I am sure we all have our scars to bear, some more openly than others.' Her gaze moved to the fireplace as she picked up her glass and took a sip of her wine.

'Do you?' Zachary continued to study her profile through narrowed lids.

She straightened her spine but continued to look

towards the fireplace rather than at him. 'Of course. How can I not after the events of this past year?'

'Tell me where you have been these past nine months, Georgianna?' he prompted softly.

She gave a start—a guilty one?—as she now looked down at the food in front of her, as if seeing it for the first time. 'Should we not eat our soup before it becomes cold?'

'By all means.' Zachary nodded. 'But there is no reason why we cannot continue talking as we eat,' he added once Georgianna had raised the spoon to her lips. A spoon that shook precariously as her hand began to tremble, until she placed it carefully back beside the soup bowl. 'What are you hiding, Georgianna?' Zachary demanded sharply as he saw that nervousness.

'Nothing.'

'Do not lie to me, Georgianna.'

She drew in a ragged breath as she now looked down at the tablecloth. 'I am not hiding anything. Or rather, I am hiding, but it is not from a what but a who,' she continued so softly it was difficult for Zachary to hear her.

'Who?'

Her eyes closed. 'Rousseau, of course.'

'Why?'

She gave another involuntary shudder. 'Because I fear what he would do if he were to ever find me again.'

Zachary had absolutely no doubt that Georgianna's fear was real. He could feel it in the tension of the air surrounding them. As he could see it, in the trembling of Georgianna's body and the quivering of her lips. 'What do you have to fear from that, Georgianna?' he prompted gruffly.

'What do you care?' She turned on him fiercely, two spots of angry colour in her cheeks. 'You have not believed a single word I have said to you so far today, so why should you think I might now bare my soul to you? Just so that you might have the pleasure of ridiculing me again?'

She had a point, Zachary conceded impatiently. But could she not see how difficult it was for him to believe the things she had told him, a woman who had eloped with a known French spy?

Except it had not been confirmed that Rousseau was a spy when Georgianna eloped with him, that certain knowledge only having come later, he reminded himself.

'This conversation is not at all conducive to our digestion.' She gave a weary shake of her head. 'Perhaps it would be best if you were to lock me back in the bedchamber.'

'You have to eat, Georgianna, or you will starve yourself to death.' Zachary scowled.

Her laugh sounded bitter. 'I am harder to kill than you might imagine!'

He was taken aback by the vehemence of her tone. 'What?'

'How went your friend's wedding today?' Once again she avoided answering his question.

The whole conversation of this past half an hour

had resembled that of a sword fight, Zachary realised irritably. He would thrust. Georgianna would parry. Georgianna would thrust. He would then parry. It was frustrating, to say the least.

But her question as to how Worthing's wedding had proceeded earlier today brought forth memories of the love and pride that shone in Worthing's face as he turned to watch his beautiful bride walk down the aisle towards him. Of that same love and pride shining in Julianna's eyes as she walked without hesitation to join her handsome bridegroom at the altar, before they spoke their vows to each other. Declaring loudly and clearly, sincerely, to love and to cherish each other from this day forward.

A bittersweet reminder to Zachary that he could never hope to have that love and devotion bestowed upon him.

And bringing into sharp contrast the wedding which should have taken place the previous year. Between a bridegroom who was only marrying because he was in need of a wife to provide his heir and to retain his fortune. And the young and romantic woman who had feared her bridegroom so much she had eloped with another man.

Zachary looked at that young woman now, once again acknowledging that he was partly, if not wholly, to blame for Georgianna having run away from her family and her home.

And for the things that had happened to her since.

Whatever they might be.

Whatever they might be?

He drew his breath in sharply. 'I believe I owe you an apology, Georgianna.'

She gave him a startled glance. 'I don't...?'

'For the manner of my proposal to you last year,' Zachary continued grimly. 'Worthing's wedding today made me see that I was unfair to you then. That I should never have spoken to your father regarding a marriage between you and I before we knew each other better.'

'We did not know each other at all!'

He nodded. 'And for that I apologise.'

Georgianna stared up at him wordlessly for several seconds, those violet-coloured eyes searching his face. 'Do not be kind to me, Zachary, please,' she finally choked out. 'I believe I can bear anything but your kindness.' She stood up to cross the room on slippered feet, coming to a halt beside the fireplace, her head bowed, revealing the vulnerable arch of her nape.

Zachary rose more slowly to his feet, more inwardly pleased than he cared to contemplate, at hearing Georgianna use his name for the first time.

He crossed the room silently until he stood just behind her, not quite touching, but enough to feel the warmth of her body just inches away. 'My actions then were selfish and totally without thought for how you might have felt in regard to marrying me. For that I am deeply sorry.' His apology still sounded awkward. As evidence, perhaps, that it did not come easily to him?

As it did not. Zachary was unable to remember the

last time he had apologised to anyone for anything he had said or done.

Georgianna's shoulders moved as she sobbed quietly. 'It does not matter any more, Zachary.'

He reached out to lightly grasp the tops of her arms. 'It does matter if it forced you into unnecessary anger towards your father and consequently into a course of action you might otherwise not have taken—' He broke off as the door opened quietly and Hinds stood uncertainly in the doorway. 'I will ring when I need you.' Zachary dismissed him grimly, waiting until the butler had left again before resuming the conversation. 'Is that what happened, Georgianna? Was it my selfishness that pushed you into taking the step of defying your father, leaving your family, and eloping with Rousseau?'

'What does it matter?' She shook her head. 'What is done cannot now be undone.'

'Georgianna.' His hands slid down the length of her arms until he clasped the bareness of both her hands in his. 'What the—?' Zachary turned her to face him before looking down to where he held her hands palms up in both of his, noting how red and roughened the skin was, with several calluses at the base of her fingers on both hands.

Georgianna almost laughed at the shocked expression on Hawksmere's face as he looked down at her work-worn hands. Except it was no laughing matter. 'They are not as pretty as they once were, are they?' She grimaced, knowing her hands were no longer those of a pampered and cosseted lady.

Zachary ran his thumbs across the calluses. 'How did this happen?'

Georgianna had learnt this past few dangerous months that it was best, whenever possible, to keep to the truth as much as possible. Far less chance of making a mistake that way. 'After André had… After he made it clear he did not want me any more, I left Paris for a while.' She raised her chin determinedly as she pulled her hands from his. 'I was lucky enough to be taken in by a kindly farmer and his wife.'

'And they obviously used you like a workhorse.' Hawksmere scowled his displeasure.

'Not at all.' Georgianna smiled slightly. 'I did work for them, of course; I could not accept their hospitality without repaying them in some small way. But it was never hard labour, just—just milking cows and feeding chickens and such. And Madame Bernard taught me how to cook. Stews, mainly. I think because…' Georgianna drew in a breath. 'They had a daughter, but she had married the year before and gone off with her soldier husband. I think they were pleased to have a young woman about the place again. In any case, they allowed me to stay with them for almost two months, after which time I decided I should return to Paris.'

'Why, when you were so obviously safe and with people who cared for you?'

She shrugged. 'I decided that I was behaving the coward by hiding away in the countryside and might be of more help to England if I were to return to the city and keep my ears and eyes open to the plots and intrigues that so abounded there. I found a job working in a tavern.'

'A tavern!' Hawksmere repeated, obviously more shocked than ever.

'In the kitchen, preparing food, rather than the tavern itself,' Georgianna assured ruefully. 'The lady who owned the tavern assured me I was not…was not buxom enough to work in the tavern itself.'

The duke raised dark brows. 'You are thinner than you were, certainly, but that does not detract… Never mind,' he said dismissively. 'I suppose this is another of those occasions when we must be grateful for small mercies?'

Georgianna smiled slightly. 'Indeed.'

'The name of this tavern?' he prompted sharply.

Georgianna had no doubt that, as she had suspected might be the case, Hawksmere would make it his business to check as to the truth of what she was now telling him. That he would not simply take her word for any of it. So, yes, better by far that she had kept to the truth as much as was possible.

Her gaze met the duke's unflinchingly. 'It was the Fleur de Lis.'

'And?' Hawksmere stilled as he looked down at her between narrowed lids. 'Surely that is the name of the tavern owned by…'

'Helene Rousseau, the sister of André Rousseau,' Georgianna confirmed evenly as she turned away to once again stare down at the fire. 'I did not go there as Georgianna Lancaster, of course, but assumed the identity of Francine Poitier, the married daughter of the farmer and his wife.' Again, she had kept to the truth as much as possible when she returned to Paris, knowing that if her identity were to be checked by Helene Rousseau, that the other woman would learn that the Bernards' did indeed have a married daughter called Francine.

Zachary released her hands to step back, not sure if he dared believe this fantastical tale. But he wanted to. Oh, yes, he found that he dearly wanted to believe it.

But, in truth, it seemed too much to accept that the young and flirtatious Georgianna Lancaster, that indulged and plump pigeon, the daughter of the Earl of Malvern, could possibly have worked as a labourer on a farm for several months, and then in the Paris tavern owned by Helene Rousseau, albeit in the kitchen. 'And how did you manage that?' he prompted in perfect French.

'I managed it very well, thank you,' Georgianna replied just as fluently. 'My father was unaware of it, of course…' she grimaced ruefully as she reverted back to English '…but during the winter months we spent at Malvern Hall before I…before I left, I had attended all of Jeffrey's French lessons with him.'

Zachary's mouth twisted humourlessly. 'No doubt drawn more by the charming and handsome Frenchman teaching the subject, than an interest in the language itself.'

'No doubt,' she conceded quietly. 'But, as you now hear, I did learn it.'

'That must have made it doubly choking for you

when the duke who offered for you was neither charming nor handsome,' he rasped harshly.

Georgianna's eyes widened incredulously. Hawksmere could not be serious, could he?

Oh, he definitely lacked the charm, was too forthright and forceful to ever be called charming, but as any woman of the *ton* would be only too happy to confirm, he was most certainly handsome. And it was a handsomeness that would cause most women to willingly overlook his lack of charm.

Even Georgianna admitted to having been taken with his dark and dangerous good looks during her first two Seasons. Indeed, he was a man it was impossible for any woman, young or old, to ignore. His arrogant bearing was always shown to advantage in his perfectly tailored clothes and she had never been able to decide whether his face was that of a fallen angel or a devil. André had possessed the face and golden hair of an angel, of course, but as Georgianna knew to her cost, he was most certainly a devil.

Whereas Zachary Black had long been considered the catch of any Season.

It had been the fact that Georgianna had been the unlikely one to 'catch' him which had come as such an unpleasant shock to her ten months ago.

Gazing at such a handsome and unobtainable duke from afar was one thing—being informed he was to become her future husband was something else completely. Even the thoughts of becoming the wife of such a cynical and experienced gentleman had thrown

Georgianna into a turmoil of doubt and fears. Mainly fears, she now realised.

What could a young girl of nineteen know of being married to a jaded gentleman of one and thirty? How would she even know what to talk to him about, let alone perform any of her other wifely duties? Georgianna had shied away from even thinking of the two of them in bed together, she plump and inexperienced, he as sleek and beautiful as a Greek god, with a legendary number of women known to have shared his bed.

Nor did she understand why he had chosen her at all, when he had never so much as even spoken or danced with her. The reason had become obvious, of course, and Hawksmere had confirmed it earlier today when he admitted he had believed her to be young enough, malleable enough, to make him an undemanding duchess.

She clasped her hands tightly together as she forced her gaze to meet his. 'So there you have the answer to your earlier question. Working in Helene Rousseau's tavern was inadvertently the way in which I gathered the information I gave you earlier.'

Impossible as it seemed, Zachary had already guessed that might be the case. Although he still had to question whether the delivery of that information had been deliberate or accidental. 'And why did you find it so difficult to confide that to me earlier?'

She drew in a deep breath. 'Because I feared you would not believe me.'

He raised dark brows. 'But you no longer fear that might be the case?'

She grimaced. 'Whether I do or I do not is no longer relevant—having now lost my liberty, I consider I have nothing else left to lose, and everything to gain, by confiding all to you.'

His eyes narrowed. 'And you expect me to believe that Helene Rousseau confided in you, a young woman she had employed to work in her kitchen?'

'Of course I do not.' Georgianna gave him an impatient glance for the derision in his tone. 'The truth is that I eavesdropped on the conversation in which Napoleon's liberation from Elba was discussed.'

'Eavesdropped how?'

'I quickly realised that a group of men, including André, met upstairs in a room of the tavern several times a week. And I discovered, quite by accident, that a convenient knothole in the floor of that room allowed their conversation to be overheard in the storeroom directly below.'

'You will have to forgive my scepticism, Georgianna.'

'Will I?' she retorted sharply.

Zachary grimaced. 'The Rousseaus, both brother and sister, have been watched constantly since it was discovered that André Duval was actually André Rousseau, a known spy for Bonaparte.'

'I am gratified to hear it,' she responded tartly. 'Indeed, it is a pity his duplicity was not discovered earlier, as it might then have saved me from considerable heartache.'

And Zachary was not in the least gratified to hear that Rousseau's treatment of her had succeeded in breaking Georgianna's heart. 'You speak now of having a fear of meeting Rousseau again; how is it that you did not fear meeting him again at his sister's tavern?'

She shook her head. 'He was present at all of those meetings, but ordinarily he had no reason to ever enter the kitchen.'

'Even so, you were taking a huge risk, Georgianna.'

'Have you never heard that it is easier to hide in full view than it is to run away and attempt to hide?' She sighed heavily.

It was a ploy Zachary had used several times himself these past four troubled years. 'I have, yes.'

'Besides, you only have to look at me now…' Georgianna glanced down ruefully at her slenderness '…to see I am nothing like the girl I once was.'

Because she was no longer a girl but a woman, Zachary conceded grimly. Beautiful, intelligent, confident, capable, but most of all, in spite of everything, utterly desirable.

And nothing Georgianna had told him this evening had lessened the pounding of the relentless desire Zachary had felt for her since meeting her again. Was it only a matter of hours ago? It seemed as if he had been in this state of constant arousal for days rather than just hours.

He gave a shake of his head in an attempt to clear his head, at least, of that desire; his body was another matter entirely. 'You understand I shall need time to confirm this new information?'

She held herself up proudly as she nodded. 'I expected nothing less.'

Zachary gave an inward groan at the way the straightening of Georgianna's spine had now pushed her breasts up against the soft material of the lilac gown. They were full and pert breasts, the nipples resembling ripe berries. As her waist would be slender, her hips gently curving, with a tempting triangle of dark curls hiding the succulent fruit between her…

'Zachary?'

'Say my name again,' he encouraged gruffly.

Georgianna blinked, taken aback by this sudden change of subject.

More than taken aback when she realised Hawksmere was now standing so close to her she could once again feel the heat of his body through the material of her gown.

Her heart began to pound rapidly in her chest as she found herself unable to look away from the fierce intensity of those mesmerising silver eyes.

Chapter Six

'Zachary, I do not...'

'Yes,' he murmured with satisfaction, his eyes glittering down at her intently as he stepped even closer to her, his thighs almost touching hers as he raised a hand to cup one of her cheeks. 'Say it again, Georgianna,' he encouraged huskily as his thumb moved caressingly across her lower lip.

She flicked her tongue out with the intention of moistening her suddenly dry lips, quickly withdrawing it again as she inadvertently caught the edge of Zachary's thumb, instantly able to taste the tangy salty sweetness of his skin. 'Zachary,' she protested weakly.

His thumb was a rousing caress in the tiny indentation in the centre of the fullness of her bottom lip. 'Are you wearing the white silk drawers tonight, Georgianna? The ones with the little lilac bows?'

Georgianna was so lost in the burning heat of that silver gaze that it took several seconds for her to realise exactly what Zachary had said. Her cheeks blushed a fiery red as she acknowledged the intimacy of his question. 'How did you know about…? You were responsible for packing my things earlier,' she said, remembering in embarrassed consternation.

He gave a feral grin. 'And I have been imagining you wearing those drawers ever since.'

Georgianna breathed shallowly. Zachary's close proximity, and that caressing thumb against her lip, made it difficult for her to think, let alone breathe.

'And the matching camisole,' he continued softly, his breath a warm caress as he lowered his head, his lips a light caress against the warmth of her throat. 'Are you wearing them both tonight, Georgianna?'

His feather-light kisses burned an arousing path down the length of her throat to the sensitive hollows beneath. Georgianna was barely breathing at all now, her hands moving up to grasp his muscled shoulders even as she arched her neck into that sensuous caress. 'Zachary, you have to stop,' she attempted half-heartedly.

'Why must I?' His hands moved down to her hips, moulding the softness of her curves against his much harder ones as his tongue dipped moistly and then withdrew from those hollows at the base of her throat, sending shivers of pleasure down the length of her spine. 'We are neither of us is involved with anyone else. Are we?'

'No.' The heat coursed through her body, tightening her breasts under her gown and camisole, warming between her thighs beneath her drawers, only the soft sighs of their ragged breathing now to charge the air. It made it impossible for Georgianna to think of a single reason why Zachary should stop.

That Zachary was equally affected was apparent by his ragged breathing and the throbbing length of his desire as his thighs pressed along the welcoming softness of her abdomen.

'Are you wearing them, Georgianna?' he pressed gruffly.

'I am, yes,' she confirmed softly, her legs feeling so weak now she was sure that if she were not clinging to the firmness of Zachary's shoulders she might find herself sinking down on to the carpeted floor at his feet.

She truly felt in danger of doing exactly that, as Zachary continued to lick and taste the length of her throat even as one of his hands slowly skimmed along the length of her hip and waist before cupping beneath the firm fullness of her breast. Her nipple instantly responded, swelling, engorging beneath the thin material of her gown and camisole in reaction to that caressing heat.

This was madness.

Complete madness.

And yet Georgianna had no strength to stop it. No will to pull away from Zachary. From the pleasure created by his lips and hands. From the closeness of him. From feeling wanted, held, for the first time in months.

And that was all this was, Georgianna told herself firmly. A need, an ache, to feel wanted and to be held. 'Have you forgotten I might be a spy?' She sought desperately for a return to sanity.

Zachary raised his head to look at her with mercurial grey eyes. There was a flush to the hardness of his cheeks and the darkness of his hair was dishevelled. 'I have forgotten nothing, Georgianna,' he assured huskily. 'If anything, I find that edge of danger only makes you more intriguing. Besides which, if you are a spy, then you are currently an imprisoned one. My imprisoned spy.' He smiled his satisfaction with that fact.

Georgianna drew her breath in sharply as she once again felt the soft pad of his thumb caress across the hardened tip of her breast.

'Perhaps that was my plan all along?' She tried to fight the sensations currently bombarding her senses: pleasure, arousal, heat. 'Has it not occurred to you that maybe my plan is to stab you at the dinner table with a knife from your own ducal-silver dinner service?' she persisted breathlessly even as she found it impossible not to arch once again into that marauding mouth as it continued to plunder the sensitive column of her throat.

'No.' Zachary smiled against the fluttering wildness of the pulse in her throat. He might have become slightly blasé this past few months, but he was nevertheless positive his self-defence skills were still as sharp. 'Because I very much doubt you will find the opportunity. Or, if you did, that my strength would not far outweigh your own.'

'Then perhaps it is my intention to hide one of the

knives and take it back upstairs with me, so that I can stab you later, while you sleep?' There was now an edge of desperation to Georgianna's voice; she simply couldn't allow this to continue.

Zachary deftly released the first button at the throat of her gown. 'Then I will have to ensure that the door between our two bedchambers remains locked at night.'

'I do not believe you are taking me seriously.'

'When I am holding you in my arms and about to kiss you? No, you may be assured I am not taking your threats seriously at all, Georgianna,' he acknowledged gruffly.

'Zachary!'

'Georgianna,' he chided gently as he released the second button and revealed the top of the silky smooth skin above the swell of her breasts.

'I cannot… This is not—' She broke off abruptly as Zachary claimed her mouth with his and silenced her protest.

She tasted as delicious as she smelt, of honey and roses, and everything that was so sweetly, temptingly Georgianna.

Zachary groaned low in his throat as he deepened the kiss, his hands sliding down the length of her spine to cup the sweet curve of her bottom and pull her closer against him, the length of his arousal nestling into the heated welcome of her abdomen.

Georgianna could not think, could only continue to cling to the strength of Zachary's shoulders as the firmness of his mouth now claimed, devoured, her own.

She felt dizzy, light-headed, as her body burned, a heated dampness moistening between her thighs as Zachary cupped the rounded globes of her bottom and held her firmly into and against him. Her breasts were crushed to the hardness of Zachary's muscled chest, the length of his erection pounding, pulsing, to the same rhythm as his heart beating so erratically against hers as his hands now roamed restlessly up the length of her spine.

A need, a want, a desire Georgianna became totally lost in. Until she felt the warmth of one of Zachary's hands against the bare skin at her throat and then lower still as he cupped the bareness of her breast beneath the material of her gown.

Her emotions immediately turned to one of panic as she realised that Zachary must have unfastened all the buttons down the front of her gown as they kissed, the material now gaping wide and revealing everything.

She wrenched her mouth from beneath his, both her hands moving up to push him aside as she pulled the sides of her gaping gown back over her chest, before glaring up at him accusingly. 'You will stop this immediately!'

His eyes narrowed to silver slits, that flush still to his cheeks and his hair dishevelled on his brow. 'Why?'

'Because I cannot allow this. It is…' Georgianna gave a shake of her head, feeling as if she were floundering, much like a fish newly hooked on the line and brought to shore. A fact Zachary was wholly aware of, if the mocking challenge in those silver eyes was any indication. And she had no doubt that it was. 'Because I do not want you,' she spat out determinedly as she hastily refastened the buttons on her gown.

'All evidence to the contrary, my dear Georgianna.' Zachary's insolent gaze moved slowly over her flushed face, slightly swollen lips, and then down the length of her throat and chest to where her nipples still pushed against the fabric of her gown.

Geogianna's lips firmed as she determinedly refused to follow the direction of that insolent gaze. 'That is purely a physical reaction to a man's touch. Any man's touch,' she added defiantly as he appeared satisfied at the admission. 'I assure you, my intellect tells me something else completely.'

'Intellect has very little to do with physical arousal,' he allowed disgustedly, all humour now gone. 'If it did, then I should not find myself in the least aroused by you, either.'

Georgianna flinched inwardly at the deliberate insult. 'Then we are in agreement on the subject, because my head tells me I should not allow a man such as you to take liberties.'

'A man such as me?'

She met his gaze defiantly. 'A libertine who is not to be trusted.'

Humour lit Zachary's eyes as he stepped back to regard her through narrowed lids. Admiration, too, because Georgianna Lancaster was, without a doubt, now a woman he could admire. Oh, not for her political beliefs, if indeed she should turn out to be a Trojan Horse for Rousseau's cause, but most definitely for the courage she had shown in the face of her present dilemma.

She was a woman who believed herself disgraced in English society. A woman who had nevertheless returned to England, only to now find herself a prisoner of the very gentleman she had once been betrothed to. Her suggestion earlier that it might have been deliberate on her part was, Zachary was sure, completely untrue; Georgianna had been far too genuinely shocked and outraged at finding herself incarcerated in his home for it to have been her intention all along.

And this, taking advantage of Georgianna, making love to her, when she was a prisoner in his home, was not a gentlemanly thing for him to do.

Georgianna's past behaviour might render her undeserving of such consideration on his part, but that did not mean he had to lose all honour.

Most especially when he still had no idea, as yet, as to whether or not Georgianna was merely Rousseau's minion, sent to England, to Zachary, at the other man's bidding.

The fact that she was now repelling his advances was, perhaps, a mark in her favour; a devious and manipulative woman would surely have used his obvious attraction to her own advantage?

Georgianna Lancaster was more than just a fully mature woman now, Zachary acknowledged, she was also an intriguing one. One who appealed to him on several levels. In her character. Intellectually. And certainly physically.

Which was all the more reason for him to keep his distance, at least until after he had confirmed, one way or the other, as to whether or not she was telling him the truth.

And if her information should prove correct, then he might no longer be given a choice about keeping his distance, because Georgianna would want nothing more to do with him after the way he had treated her whilst holding her prisoner.

His mouth twisted mockingly. 'It takes one to know one, my dear Georgianna.'

Georgianna gasped, her face paling at what she knew to be another deliberately delivered insult and a direct reference to her scandalous behaviour the previous year. 'I believe I will go back upstairs to my room now.'

'You have not eaten any dinner.'

'I am not hungry.'

The duke's lips firmed with his displeasure. 'It is no wonder you are now thin as a stick, if you do not eat.'

Georgianna refused, absolutely refused, to spill the heat of tears that now blurred her vision. 'You did not seem to have any complaints a few minutes ago, your Grace,' she reminded stiffly.

He shrugged wide shoulders. 'Thankfully the size of your breasts does not seem to have suffered in the process.'

Colour now burned Georgianna's cheeks. 'You are truly insufferable.'

He raised dark brows. 'Was that ever in any doubt?'

'Obviously not.' She blinked back those tears as she lowered her lashes before turning away, no longer willing to even look at that triumphantly mocking face. 'If you would care to act the turnkey again, I am more than ready to return to my room.'

Zachary cursed himself for feeling every kind of monster as he gazed upon the stiff slenderness of Georgianna's back and the vulnerability of her exposed nape, knowing he could not give in to the impulse he felt to take her back into his arms and apologise for having deliberately insulted her.

For having hurt her?

Her eyes had looked awash with tears again before she lowered those long, protective lashes, as if his cutting words really had injured her feelings.

Damn it, how long could it take to confirm or deny Georgianna's information? Zachary wondered impatiently. How much longer did he have to wait before he…?

Before he what? Exactly what difference was it going to make to Zachary's dealings with Georgianna once he did know the truth?

Georgianna might have responded to him a short time ago, but she also so obviously despised him, and herself, for that response. He could not see anything, even the unlikely confirmation of her information being true, ever changing that.

'Very well.' Zachary nodded abruptly, having no

appetite himself now. For dinner, at least. 'But a dinner tray will be brought up to your room.'

Her head remained bowed as she nodded. 'Thank you.'

'And you will eat its contents,' he added sternly.

Humour glinted in her eyes as she looked across at him. 'Must I remind you that your dictates to me so far have not proved in the least successful?'

No, Zachary needed no reminding of Georgianna's wilfulness. Or of his own response to those displays of stubbornness. 'That is because you are contrary in the extreme.'

'That being the case, perhaps you should have instructed me not to eat the food on the dinner tray rather than to eat it?'

'That would be a useless exercise now that we have discussed the possibility,' Zachary dismissed impatiently. 'Eat, or do not eat,' he advised wearily. 'Personally, I grew bored with the subject some minutes ago.'

As Georgianna had no doubt he was bored with having her in his home. With her. And who could blame him? It was so obviously not his choice, but had been foisted upon him by his superior. As she had been foisted on him.

Zachary could not really be blamed for having tried to lighten that burden by entertaining himself in making love to her. A woman whose intimate association with another man put her well beyond the need for either respect or maidenly consideration from the top-lofty Duke of Hawksmere.

She straightened her shoulders. 'Then I will relieve you of the necessity of suffering any more boredom by removing myself from your presence, so allowing you to go out and seek more entertaining and exciting company.'

Frustration surged inside Zachary as he eyed her impatiently, knowing he did not find Georgianna in the least boring. Indeed, she continued to intrigue and entertain him in a way he could not remember feeling with any other woman. Nor could he recall ever being anywhere near as 'excited' by another woman, as he had been just from kissing and caressing Georgianna.

He gave a mocking inclination of his head. 'That is very considerate of you.'

'I thought so, too,' she riposted drily.

Georgianna's sense of humour so appealed to his own that Zachary knew if he did not have a care he would find himself laughing once again, a move guaranteed to completely nullify the distance that he had deliberately put between them this past few minutes. It was a distance Zachary knew he desperately needed to maintain if he were to continue to keep the upper hand with this particular woman. If, indeed, he still had it. If he had ever had it?

Georgianna's flight from a marriage to him ten months ago would seem to imply, that even as the flirtatious and slightly immature Lady Georgianna Lancaster, she had possessed a wilfulness that had been strong enough to at least ensure the unwanted marriage did not take place. The Georgianna who had returned from France was even more determined to defy, and alternately beguile, him at every turn.

Zachary held himself stiffly. 'Luckily I do not need your permission to do anything I wish, or go anywhere I please, whereas the same obviously cannot be said of you.' He eyed her challengingly.

Rebellion glowed in those violet-coloured eyes. 'The bedchamber you have allocated for my use is far superior to my lodgings at Mrs Jenkins's house. It also has the added advantage of being given to me completely free of charge.'

Experience, so far in their reacquaintance, had served to show Zachary that it was doubtful he would ever manage to have the last word in a conversation with this particular woman. 'That could change at any moment,' he drawled challengingly in an attempt to do so.

Her chin rose stubbornly as she met that challenge. 'Your threats grow as wearisome to me as my company has become boring to you.'

The smile refused to be denied this time as Zachary gave a weary, defeated shake of his head. His lack of sleep the night before was certainly taking its toll on him now. A disadvantage Georgianna obviously did not suffer from. 'I do believe your tenacity of will has worn me down for this evening, Georgianna.'

'I am glad to hear it,' she replied pertly. 'Now, if you will excuse me? I really would prefer to return to my room.'

And Zachary, much as he might prefer to go out for the rest of the evening, well away from the temptation of knowing Georgianna was in the bedchamber adjoining his own, now knew himself to be so tired, from lack of sleep and the exhaustion of constantly crossing verbal swords with Georgianna, that he wanted nothing more than to go to his own bedchamber and sleep like the dead for a dozen hours or more.

He nodded abruptly. 'I will arrange for Hinds to bring you up a tray of food shortly.'

She arched one dark brow. 'Do you not intend to lock me in again first?'

He smiled slightly. 'I believe Hinds may find it rather difficult to deliver your tray if the door is locked.'

'And if I should attempt to escape in the meantime?'

Zachary took two predatory steps forward, coming to a halt just inches in front of Georgianna and forcing her to tilt her head back in order to look up at him.

'If you were to escape, Georgianna, then I should then have the pleasure of tracking you down,' he told her softly. 'And when I had, you may be assured I should extract the necessary revenge for your having dared to defy me.'

Georgianna repressed a shiver of apprehension as she saw the raw intensity of emotion glittering in the hard depths of Zachary's eyes. Challenge. Confidence. Amusement.

It was the latter emotion that caused her to straighten resentfully. 'You would have to find me first. Something I believe you were not too successful in doing ten months ago,' she added with deliberate sweetness.

His lids narrowed about those silver eyes. 'Perhaps that is because I did not bother to look too hard for my obviously reluctant bride?'

Colour warmed her cheeks. 'As you had never so much as bothered even speaking to her, I am not surprised. Indeed, as I have already told you, my only surprise is that you haven't found my replacement and married since.'

Zachary looked down at her coldly, only too well aware that his time for marrying, and producing an heir, was ticking by faster than he would have wished. 'Perhaps that is because I have decided to be more cautious in my second attempt at matrimony.'

'How sad to know you were the second choice for the Duke of Hawksmere's duchess!' she retorted tartly.

He drew in a sharp breath. 'My wife will not be my second choice, but the correct one. Which you, most assuredly, were not.'

The colour deepened in Georgianna's cheeks. 'Then it appears we may both be thankful for having escaped such an ill-matched union.'

'Indeed, we can,' Zachary bit out harshly.

They stared each other down for several more long seconds before Georgianna turned sharply on her heel and walked hastily from the room.

Much as he might wish to, Zachary did not trouble himself in following her, knowing he was in no mood at the moment to deal with her gently. Besides, he had meant it when he said he would very much enjoy the pleasure of recapturing her, and extracting payment, if she should try to escape Hawksmere House.

And him.

Chapter Seven

'It is past time you woke up, Georgianna.'

Georgianna roused slowly from the deepness of her slumbers at the sound of that intruding voice. She'd been sleeping so deeply, lost in a most wonderful dream. A dream where she had felt both safe and warm, something she had not been for so very long.

'Georgianna!'

She frowned as the impatient voice rallied her for a second time. She was so very reluctant to relinquish those feelings of safety after months of fear and the nervousness of discovery.

'If you do not open your eyes in the next few seconds, Georgianna, then you will leave me with no choice but to throw this jug of cold water over you.'

It really was Hawksmere talking to her, she realised with a groan.

For surely only Zachary Black, the forceful Duke of Hawksmere, could be so very demanding? So impatient for her to obey his every instruction, he threatened to douse her in water?

She forced her lids to open before going up on her elbows to seek his exact location in the half gloom of the bedchamber. 'What? That was deliberately cruel.' She glowered across the room at the duke as she saw he stood beside where he had just thrown back the curtains fully in order to let in the brightness of the morning's sunshine.

He gave a hard and unapologetic smile. 'But no doubt preferable to the dousing in cold water. Of course, the water for washing was not cold when it was delivered to your room three hours ago,' he added scathingly. 'But it most certainly will be now.'

Three hours ago? 'What time is it?' Georgianna pushed the silky curtain of her hair over her shoulders.

Hawksmere strode impatiently to the bedside, revealing he was already dressed for the day, in a dark grey superfine, silver brocade waistcoat over white linen, with pale grey pantaloons and brown-topped Hessians. 'After eleven.'

Georgianna blinked up at him. After eleven o'clock in the morning? Then she had must have slept for a dozen hours or more after eating a little of the food from the tray that Hinds had delivered to her room last evening. How could she have slept for so long? It had been weeks, months, since she had been able to sleep so deeply.

She recalled her dream. The safety and the warmth she had felt cocooning her. Implying she felt safe in

Hawksmere's home? With Hawksmere just feet away in the adjoining bedchamber? The same gentleman who had threatened and imprisoned her? Impossible!

And yet...

Georgianna could not deny that she had felt that sense of safety and warmth as she awoke, as if nothing and no one could harm her whilst she was in Hawksmere House.

A feeling she had no intentions of sharing with Hawksmere himself.

'Obviously you slept well,' he added mockingly. 'No doubt you will claim it was the sleep of the innocent.'

Georgianna frowned at his harshness, checking that her nightgown was securely fastened up to her throat before sitting up in the bed to glare accusingly at her tormentor. 'You should have woken me earlier if my sleeping late displeases you.'

He raised dark brows. 'I do not believe that is included in my duties, as your gaoler.'

'Then perhaps in future it should be,' she snapped irritably.

Hawksmere frowned grimly 'I have had other things to occupy me this morning, other than troubling myself to wake you from your lazy slumbers.'

Georgianna almost laughed at his words; there had been no lazy slumbers for her since she'd left England for France the previous year!

The time she had spent with André had been rife with tension and the days had started early on the Barnards' farm. The tavern had been even worse, with late nights cooking food followed by early mornings spent cleaning in readiness for the next influx of customers.

All so very unlike her previous pampered and privileged life as the only daughter of the Earl of Malvern.

She looked up at Hawksmere searchingly now, immediately noting the grimness about his eyes and the firmness of his mouth. His expression was altogether one of harshness this morning, rather than the lazy mockery he had shown towards her yesterday evening. His movements were restless as he turned away from the bed and began to pace the bedchamber.

'What other things have occupied you this morning?' she prompted warily.

Zachary shot her an impatient glance, not sure how much he should reveal to Georgianna, how much he needed to reveal to her, when the information delivered to him earlier this morning was not confirmed, only suspected at this point in time. When his instructions were still to keep her a prisoner here.

He drew in a controlling breath. 'I shall be leaving London later today and I am uncertain when I shall return.'

'You are leaving London?' she echoed sharply. 'To go where?'

Zachary had known that Georgianna was too intelligent, had grown too unconventional in her ways, to accept his statement without suspicion or question, as most women in society would have done. To most women a gentleman's activities outside their home were his own affair and definitely not to be questioned too deeply. Not so with the forthright Georgianna, unfortunately.

He glowered down at her, wishing she did not look quite so delectable this morning, her face soft and flushed from sleep, that silky dark hair once again loose about her shoulders and down her spine. The white cotton nightgown also did little to hide the fact that she was naked beneath it, her breasts jutting out firm and tempting against its voluptuous folds.

'What will you do with me while you are away?' she added slowly.

Zachary scowled. 'You will remain here, of course.'

Her eyes widened. 'You intend leaving me a prisoner in this bedchamber indefinitely?'

'I see no alternative.' Much as he might wish it were otherwise. And the thought of keeping Georgianna cooped up in this bedchamber was not a pleasant one. Especially when he had no idea how long her incarceration would last. Or when he would return to England.

'Where are you going, Zachary?' she demanded sharply. 'Tell me,' she insisted determinedly as his mouth thinned.

He sighed his impatience as he once again wished for a less intelligent and astute woman than Georgianna. 'As you are to remain incarcerated here, I can see no harm in your knowing that rumours have reached our shores that Napoleon is on the move.'

'I knew it!' Georgianna announced, her face aglow with triumph as she threw back the bedcovers before climbing out of the bed and revealing that her nightgown covered her from her throat down to her slender ankles.

Or it attempted to do so, because Zachary could clearly make out the shadowy outline of the rosy tips to the fullness of her breasts, as well as the dark shadow of the curls nestled so seductively between her thighs.

He gave an inward groan as his own body instantly reacted to those tantalising glimpses of the shadowy outline of Georgianna's body, his arousal hardening to pulsing need inside his pantaloons.

'Did I not tell you it would be so, Zachary?' she continued excitedly, her face glowing with that excitement as she paced quickly to one of the windows, unknowingly allowing the sun, as it shone through the glass, to instantly turn her nightgown diaphanous.

Zachary closed his eyes briefly in order to shut out the sight of Georgianna's slender nakedness so clearly outlined through the white material. A brief visual respite that made absolutely no difference to the engorging of his erection as it continued to pulse, to lengthen and thicken, with impatient need.

He gave a shake of his head as he opened his lids to look across at her guardedly. 'Has no one ever told you it is most unattractive to say *I told you so* in that triumphant manner?'

'Hah to that.' Georgianna was too excited at being proved right to behave in the least ladylike about it, despite Hawksmere's rebuke. 'I was right, Zachary, and you were wrong, and you may mock all you like, but…' She stilled, excitement dying as she took in the full import of Hawksmere's statement. 'He is already on the move, you say?'

The duke gave a haughty inclination of his head. 'So it is reported, yes.'

'Then I was too late to be of help, after all.' Georgianna groaned, shoulders slumping in defeat. 'I delayed too long and arrived too late, Zachary.' She buried her face in her hands. 'Too late.'

Zachary was instantly torn between the need to go to Georgianna and comfort her by taking her into his arms, and the certain knowledge that if he did so he would be unable to stop himself from making love to her again. Last night had been a tortuous hell for him after he and Georgianna had parted so ignominiously. Knowing Georgianna was in the adjoining bedchamber, that silky ebony hair no doubt once again loose about her shoulders and breasts, and wearing nothing more than one of the two white nightgowns he had packed into her bag earlier in the day at her lodgings, had played havoc with his efforts to find rest, let alone sleep.

So much so that he had quickly worked himself up into a fine temper, his annoyance with both Georgianna, and his own weakness in desiring her, making it impossible for him to relax.

He had finally given up all attempt of sleeping just before two o'clock in the morning. He'd thrown back the bedcovers to get out of bed and pull on his brocade robe over his nakedness before pacing about his bedchamber instead. All the time aware, so totally aware, that Georgianna was just a door-width away from satisfying the lust that coursed so hotly through his body.

A lust Zachary could not, dare not, allow to rule him, when he still distrusted the woman responsible for that emotion.

Only to then realise, when Georgianna had slept in so late this morning, that while he had been suffering the torments of the damned the night before, she had been perfectly at peace in the adjoining bedchamber, sleeping like the dead—or innocent?—and so totally unaware of his own tormented longings.

His visitor earlier this morning, bearing news of Napoleon's possible flight from Elba, had done nothing to improve the already short fuse on his overstretched temper. To so much as touch her now would be insanity on his part.

Oh, to hell with his caution, Zachary dismissed as he took the two long strides that brought him to her side, before reaching out to take her in his arms. He wanted this woman, to kiss her, to caress her, and God knew when he would have the opportunity to do so again.

She was so very slight, in both height and stature. Her head rested against his chest just beneath his chin. So slender, it was almost like holding a child in his arms.

Almost.

Because it was a certainty that Georgianna did not bring out even a spark of paternal instinct in him.

'I should not have delayed my departure from France for so long.' Her voice was muffled against his chest, her breath a warm caress through the thin material of his shirt. 'Should not have been so cautious, so worried, that I might be discovered attempting to leave. And now Napoleon will return to France and— My God—' she lifted her head to look up at Zachary searchingly, her face paling as realisation dawned '—that is where you are going, is it not?'

It so happened that that was exactly where Zachary was going.

But he was not allowed to discuss his mission. Even with the woman who was responsible for bringing him the news that it was Napoleon's intention to leave Elba. If, as was suspected, the Corsican had not already done so.

Zachary gave a mocking smile. 'I had not realised you had such a vivid imagination, Georgianna.'

'Do not even attempt to treat me like the foolish young girl I once was, Zachary,' Georgianna warned fiercely.

His expression was grim. 'Oh, I assure you, I am only too well aware that you are no longer that young innocent, Georgianna, foolish or otherwise.'

'Then do not… Umph!' The last came out as a protesting squeak as Zachary silenced her by claiming her mouth with his own, his arms like steel bands about her waist as he held her so tightly to him her body was melded close against his own.

Georgianna fought against the confinement of those arms as she also tried to wrench her mouth from beneath his. All to no avail, as Zachary merely tightened his arms and deepened the kiss by parting her lips beneath his with the invasion of his tongue into the moist heat of her mouth.

His marauding tongue that explored every sensitive and heated contour of her mouth, before stilling her as that tongue stroked against her own in a slow and sensuous caress, claiming, possessing, and sending rivulets of pleasurable heat coursing through the whole of Georgianna's body.

She had never… No one had ever made her feel like this before.

The sheer carnality of Zachary's kiss was beyond anything Georgianna had ever experienced before, beyond anything she had ever imagined, and she had no defences against it.

No defence against Zachary as he continued to plunder and claim her mouth even as he lifted her up into his arms and carried her across the room to lay her down upon the bed before joining her there. He draped one of his legs across her thighs to keep her in place beside him as he continued to kiss and taste her even while one of his hands began to roam restlessly along the length of her body.

Her neck arched as Zachary broke that kiss to explore the column of her throat. She gasped as his hand cupped beneath her breast, instantly seeking out the sensitive berry at its tip, caressing, stroking and causing a tingling ache that spread like wildfire from her nipple down to between her dampening thighs.

Nevertheless, she knew she must seek some semblance of sanity, to put an end to the madness that had so rapidly overtaken them. 'Zachary.'

'Do not deny the desire that exists between us, Georgianna.' He raised his head to look at her, his eyes glittering fiercely, a flush across the sharp blades of his cheekbones, his lips thinned.

As evidence that his own desire for her angered him rather than pleased him?

No doubt it did, when Zachary had every reason to believe she had been André Rousseau's lover.

'I will allow you to think of nothing and no one else whilst you are in my arms, Georgianna,' he warned harshly, as he seemed to guess some of her thoughts. 'And I fully intend to have you before I leave,' he continued determinedly as he rose above and then over her, pushing her nightgown up her thighs as he settled between her legs. 'All of you.'

She swallowed at the lustful violence she now saw in the fierceness of Zachary's gaze. A violence of emotion that threatened to overwhelm completely Zachary's previous cautions where she was concerned.

Georgianna ran the moistness of her tongue across the dryness of her lips. 'You will only regret it.'

'As you warned me yesterday I should regret having insisted you remove your veil?' he retorted harshly as he slid slowly down the length of her body, able to smell the sweet lure of her arousal once he was comfortably settled between her thighs.

'Yes.'

'And I did regret it. I regret it still. But it seems that regret does little to change the fact that I also desire you.' Zachary gave a shake of his head, his endurance, and his patience, pushed beyond his control after his second sleepless night in succession. Because of this woman. Because of the desire he felt for her. A desire he had every intention of satisfying before he left England later today.

'Please, Zachary.'

'Oh, I intend to please you, Georgianna.' He looked down as his hands moved up her thighs, pushing her nightgown up to her waist, revealing smooth, ivory skin and the dark thatch of curls nestled between her thighs. 'And by pleasing you I also intend to please myself,' he promised darkly, even as his fingers parted those curls to reveal the lushness of her rosy red folds with the little nubbin peeking out temptingly from beneath the hood above. 'Open your legs wider and let me in, Georgianna,' he encouraged gruffly.

'I cannot.'

'You can.' Zachary moved even lower, the width of his shoulders pushing her thighs further apart, and allowing the heat of his gaze to feast on the slickness of her folds. So deep and rosy coloured, the lips there already swollen, moist, with Georgianna's own arousal. 'You are so beautiful, Georgianna,' he murmured as his thumbs moved to part those folds, revealing the moist and welcoming centre. 'Like a flower unfurling petals touched by the morning dew.'

Georgianna was not sure which mortified her the most, the suddenness of this intimacy, or her unmistakable arousal. Certainly she could not deny she was aroused, but at the same time she felt embarrassed by that response. At having a man, any man, look at and touch her so intimately. To have Zachary look and touch where she had never even looked or touched herself.

'I had not taken you for a poet, Hawksmere.'

'You and this lush bounty make me one,' he assured gruffly as his fingers lightly caressed the delicacy of her skin.

'I…'

Georgianna's protest died in her throat, her back arching off the bed at the first pleasurable sweep of the heat of Zachary's moist tongue against that very private place, before he commenced a slow and sensuous licking of those sensitive folds. He greedily lapped up the moisture now flowing between her thighs.

'I do not…' Georgianna halted with a gasp as the pleasure became so intense it threatened to totally overwhelm her.

Zachary felt the deepening of Georgianna's response as his tongue now probed beneath the hood above her folds, seeking out that erect nubbin, lathing and then sucking it fully into his mouth as he felt it pulsing against his tongue as evidence of her rapidly approaching climax.

His senses were filled with the taste and smell of her, like the sweetest of nectars, and just as addictive. 'Yes, Georgianna,' he encouraged hotly as she now arched up into the stroking of his tongue. 'Find your rhythm, love. Move with me. Into me. Yes,' he muttered fiercely as she found that rhythm with the undulating arching of her hips.

He slipped a finger between the slickness of her folds, stroking the edge, before sliding slowly inside, groaning low in his throat as he added a second finger and felt her muscles tighten about him. Imagining, craving, those same muscles tightening snugly about his erection in exactly the same way they gripped his fingers.

But first he intended to pleasure Georgianna, to obliterate from her memory any other lover she had ever known.

He continued that slow thrusting with his fingers even as he lowered his head and his tongue once again stroked the erect nubbin above, suckling it into his mouth before closing his teeth gently about it.

Georgianna gasped and then cried out as the pleasure rose up to an unbearable height before crashing, streaking through her in hot, burning flames, threatening to consume her with their intensity. Wave after wave of mindless, all-consuming pleasure, tossing her higher, and then higher still as Zachary continued to stroke and thrust her to a second, even more exquisitely powerful climax with the merciless strokes of his tongue. Her body contracting as he continued to thrust his fingers deep inside that flooding heat.

'No more. Please, Zachary,' she finally cried out weakly, so sensitive now that every touch, every stroke threatened to send her over the edge of falling into yet another exquisite climax.

'Why not?' Zachary's eyes were dark as he raised his head to look up at her, his cheeks flushed.

Georgianna felt the heat burn her cheeks as she saw how glistening wet his lips were, and realised it had to be from the copious flowing of her juices. 'I had not realised... I did not know. Do men enjoy doing that?'

'I do,' Zachary assured gruffly, pleased beyond measure that he was obviously the first man to have introduced Georgianna to this intimacy. 'You taste divine, Georgianna,' he added huskily as he licked the juices from his lips and had the pleasure of watching her cheeks blush an even deeper red.

'And I—' He broke off with a scowl as a knock sounded on the door of the bedchamber. 'What is it?' He turned to direct that scowl towards that closed door.

'The Duke of Wolfingham is awaiting your presence down in the blue salon, your Grace,' Hinds informed him stiffly through the closed door.

Damn it. Zachary had completely forgotten that Wolfingham was joining him here this morning.

Forgotten everything but his need to make love to Georgianna.

Chapter Eight

Georgianna washed, and dressed herself in the black gown, then arranged her hair neatly at her crown in record time after Zachary left her bedchamber. She was determined that when, and if, the duke should return, her appearance would at least be respectable.

The only thing she now considered 'respectable' about herself.

She had no idea what had happened with Hawksmere just now. One minute they had been talking, and the next…

Oh, dear lord, the next.

Just thinking about Zachary possessing her with his mouth was enough to make Georgianna quiver with embarrassment.

Or possibly remembered pleasure?

Unimagined, indescribable, out-of-this-world pleasure.

She had not known such intimacies, such pleasure, as that existed.

The attentions of Zachary's mouth, tongue and fingers had been centred between her thighs, but the pleasure had been felt everywhere. Radiating out from between her and consuming her every sensation, as it coursed, burned through her torso and throat, and into all of her limbs to the very ends of her fingers and her toes. And not just once, but twice! That pleasure building again, carrying her along on a tide of sensation. By the time Hinds had knocked on the door of her bedchamber...

Hinds!

What must he think? What conclusion could the butler have come to, in respect of the time his employer had spent in Georgianna's bedchamber this morning?

Considering the reason Zachary had informed his household staff for her being here at all, no doubt the butler had drawn the correct conclusion regarding their activities this morning.

Georgianna was genuinely shocked at her own behaviour. Mortified. She had no idea how she was going to face Zachary again when he had looked at her and touched her so intimately.

However, this personal mortification paled into insignificance in the face of Napoleon's move from Elba.

If it was true, and if Napoleon should indeed return to the shores of France, then there was sure to be another war. England and her allies could not just sit back and allow the Corsican to retake the French crown for his own. And if, when, that happened, more Englishmen would die.

And to think, Georgianna might have prevented it if she had been more courageous. If she had not wasted so much time seeking safe and undetected passage for herself from France.

Zachary might be one of the ones to die.

Sooner rather than later if, as she suspected, he was leaving for France later today.

If Napoleon should make it back to France in the next few days, as he was bound to do, then the next few weeks, as he marched towards Paris, would be dangerous indeed. Having lived there for the past few months, Georgianna knew, perhaps better than most, that the people of France were not all enamoured of having their king returned to them. And that many, given the choice, would far rather that Napoleon return as their emperor.

The thought of Zachary deliberately placing himself in the midst of that turmoil was a frightening one.

Georgianna shied away from admitting why she found the idea of Zachary in danger so disturbing. Shied away from facing that truth. Even to herself.

She should hate Zachary Black. For having imprisoned her here. For disbelieving the things she had told him about André, as well as Napoleon's plans to leave Elba. Most certainly for the liberties he had taken with her this morning.

And yet she found she could not bring herself to hate Zachary. Certainly not enough to wish him ill. To wish him dead.

Surely she had not come to care for him this past day or so? To feel something, some nameless, softening of emotion, for the very man she had run away from marrying in the first place?

What other explanation was there for her response to him such a short time ago?

It would be worse than ironic if that should be the case.

'What are you thinking about so intently?'

Georgianna spun sharply to face the man standing in the doorway of the bedchamber. The same gentleman, who now occupied so much of her thoughts.

Her face was instantly ablaze with embarrassed colour, as she found her gaze drawn to those beautifully sculptured lips. Lips, that such a short time ago, had been kissing and suckling her intimately.

'I was merely wondering exactly when you intended leaving for France, so that I might know when I will, most thankfully, be relieved of your company,' she replied tartly, her gaze now meeting his boldly.

Zachary gave a slow and mocking smile at that now-familiar sharpness; ridiculous of him to have expected that their earlier intimacies might have in any way softened Georgianna's feelings towards him.

The fact that she had once again dressed in the unbecoming black gown in his absence was evidence enough, surely, that she regretted those intimacies?

At the same time as Zachary acknowledged he now had no choice but to believe that the information Georgianna had given him about Napoleon's movements was, in fact, the truth.

As had been her claim not to have seen Rousseau for many months?

The intelligence report that Zachary had read on Rousseau would seem to indicate that also was true.

Which, taken to its logical conclusion, must also mean that Georgianna had indeed parted from Rousseau only a week or so after arriving in France, and that she had then worked on a farm for several months, before going to back to Paris to work as a kitchen maid in Helene Rousseau's tavern.

Zachary found himself scowling at the thought of this beautiful young woman wandering alone about the French countryside, let alone returning to Paris to work in such a lowly tavern as the Fleur de Lis, leaving herself prey to any and all of that inn's patrons.

'Never mind my own plans for now, what on earth did you think you were doing by remaining in France once Rousseau had finished with you, and so putting yourself in danger for so many months?' He scowled his displeasure.

Oh, yes, André had certainly finished with her, she reflected bitterly. Indeed, as far as she was aware he still believed he had finished her off completely and that her stripped and bleached bones now lay scattered about a forest outside Paris.

She gave an uninterested shrug. 'Why not stay, when I had nothing to return to in England?'

'Your father was still alive then, and your brother…'

'A father and a brother who had quite rightly disowned me,' she responded tautly.

The duke scowled.

'Why did the Duke of Wolfingham need to speak with you so urgently?' she prompted shrewdly.

Zachary raised dark brows. 'I do not recall Hinds indicating that Wolfingham's visit was urgent in nature.'

'I assumed, from the haste with which you left earlier… Silly me.' Georgianna gave a discomforted grimace. 'No doubt the urgency was for you to leave my bedchamber, rather than your need to rush to Wolfingham.'

'And yet here I am, back again,' he drawled.

'Only because you had not finished our earlier conversation, I am sure.' Georgianna turned away to walk over to one of the windows. 'You cannot seriously intend to leave me a prisoner here whilst you go to France?'

'I do not believe I have ever confirmed my intention of going to France.'

'But we both know that you are.' Georgianna glanced back at him as he did not deny it a second time. 'And you would have admitted it was so earlier if we had not been…' Her face flushed fiery red as she remembered the reason for their earlier distraction.

'No, I would not, Georgianna, and for the simple reason I do not consider my immediate plans to be any of your concern,' Zachary bit out harshly.

Georgianna recoiled at the disdain underlying his dismissal. It was as if he had physically struck her. As if, despite everything, Zachary still distrusted her.

She turned stiffly to face him. 'Nevertheless, you

cannot expect me to continue to remain here whilst you are away.'

'And yet that is exactly what I expect.' Hawksmere eyed her challengingly.

'And if I should choose to make my presence here a difficult one?'

'Then do so by all means. It will make no difference to the outcome.' Zachary was no happier than Georgianna about the arrangement, and as such, his patience had worn beyond thin on the subject.

She raised haughty brows. 'You may be lord and master of all you survey in your own world, Zachary, but I assure you, you are not my lord or master, in this world or any other.'

No, because if he were, Zachary would have put her over his knee by now and spanked her obstinate little bottom into obedience. As it was, he was so angry with her, not just for her stubbornness now, but because he now knew she had deliberately placed herself in danger these past months. So angry that he might still be driven to that action, if Georgianna didn't cease arguing with him at every turn.

Not that he had really expected their earlier intimacy to have changed that stubbornness in any way. Georgianna had shown him only too clearly that this wilfulness was part and parcel of who she was. Or, at least, who she had become.

No doubt those weeks and months she had spent alone in France, fearing for her safety, for her life, were in part responsible for her present independence of nature.

The truth was, after the information Zachary had received this morning, he now believed the things Georgianna had told him about the time she had spent in France. And knowing that she had wilfully chosen to put herself in harm's way by working at the tavern of Helene Rousseau was enough to turn the blood cold in Zachary's veins. Anything might have happened to her; a young and beautiful woman, so obviously alone and without male protection.

As perhaps anything had?

His eyes narrowed. 'Where did you live while working in the kitchen of Helene Rousseau's tavern?'

Georgianna eyed Hawksmere warily as she heard the steely edge beneath the softness of his tone. 'I do not see that is any of your concern.'

'Answer the question, damn you.' He strode forcefully across the room.

She blinked up at him as he now stood just inches in front of her. 'I was given a room in the attic.'

'You lived on the premises?'

She nodded. 'So I was about to tell you, if you had let me finish.'

He drew in a slow and deliberate breath. 'You, Lady Georgianna Lancaster, daughter, and now sister of the Earl of Malvern, lived in the attic of a common French tavern?'

Georgianna had no idea why Hawksmere was so obviously angry on the subject. Living in the attic of the Fleur de Lis paled into insignificance when she considered the other dangers she had faced during those months in France. 'Mademoiselle Rousseau allowed me to stay there as part of my payment.'

'So that you might entertain men there?'

Georgianna gasped in shock. ' Of course not! How dare you imply—?' She broke off as Hawksmere took a painful grasp of the tops of her arms, his face tight with anger as he towered over her.

'I was employed as a kitchen maid, not a whore, Hawksmere.'

'I very much doubt that the men who frequented the tavern were capable of making that distinction.' he said scornfully.

She frowned. 'You are obviously more familiar with the practises of such places than I.'

His hands tightened painfully as he shook her. 'It is not a question of what I am familiar with.'

'Is it not?' Georgianna challenged scathingly. 'I worked in the kitchen of the tavern, Hawksmere,' she maintained firmly. 'And that is all I did.' She looked up at him defiantly.

Zachary looked down at her searchingly, seeing the challenge glittering in those violet-coloured eyes, the unmistakable pride in the tilt of her chin, indignation in the stiffness of her body. As proof of her innocence? In regard to the months she had spent working at the tavern, perhaps; the weeks she had spent as Rousseau's mistress were a different matter entirely.

'What more is it going to take for you to trust me, Zachary?' She looked up at him with pained eyes. 'You now have information that confirms Napoleon is to leave Elba, if he has not already done so. What more do you need from me to be convinced that I have told you nothing but the truth since we met again yesterday?'

His jaw tightened. 'You have yet to tell me how you escaped from Rousseau once your association was over.'

Her gaze avoided meeting his. 'Is that really necessary?'

'It is if you truly wish for me to trust you.'

She moistened dry lips. 'And if I tell you, will you then consider allowing me to leave this house at the same time you do?'

'To go where?'

'Anywhere I am not a prisoner.'

'I will consider the idea, yes,' he bit out tautly.

'That is not good cnough.'

'It is all the concession I am willing to make at this point.'

Georgianna stared up at Hawksmere's hard and unyielding expression, his eyes that glittering remorseless silver. As evidence that he would not relent without that last irrefutable proof from her as to her innocence.

She had hoped to spare herself this final humiliation, but saw now that it was not to be, that the time for such prevarication was now at an end.

'Release my arms, if you please,' she instructed softly.

Zachary looked down at her searchingly for several long seconds before his fingers slowly loosened, his hands dropping back to his sides as he took a step back.

Georgianna averted her gaze from meeting his own, her hands shaking as she raised them to the neckline of her black gown, fingers fumbling as she began to unfasten the tiny buttons.

'Georgianna, I do not have the time now to finish what we started earlier,' Hawksmere dismissed impatiently. 'Nor will you succeed in distracting me by attempting to seduce me,' he added scathingly.

'You are arrogance personified.' Georgianna's fingers paused on the buttons of her gown as she gave him a pitying glance. 'I have absolutely no intentions of distracting or attempting to seduce you.'

He raised dark brows. 'Then why are you unfastening your gown?'

She sighed heavily. 'Because it is the only way I know of to show you how I escaped from Rousseau.'

'I do not see how the unfastening of your gown will help convince me of anything.'

'Will you please cease your sarcasm for just a few moments, Hawksmere?' Georgianna's voice shook with emotion, her vision blurred by unshed tears as she looked up at him. 'I cannot—' She bit her bottom lip as she gave a shake of her head. 'I believe if I have to suffer another one of your insults then I might begin to scream and never stop.'

Zachary could see that by the strained expression on Georgianna's face. Her eyes were a dark purple and shimmering with tears, her cheeks pale and hollow, all the colour seeming to have drained even from the fullness of her lips. She was seriously distressed. Enough to scream? He believed so, yes.

'In that case, please continue,' he invited in a bored voice as he moved to slowly lower his length comfortably down on to the chair placed in front of the dressing table.

Her eyes narrowed as she glared across at him. 'I only intend to unfasten a few buttons of my gown, Hawksmere, not provide a striptease show with you as the audience.'

'That is a pity,' he drawled as he crossed one elegant leg over the other.

Georgianna closed her eyes briefly in an attempt to dig deep inside herself for the courage needed for her to continue along this course.

Not an easy feat when Hawksmere continued to treat her with such disdain. Nor was there any guarantee, having literally bared her scarred soul to him, that he would dispense once and for all with the distrust with which he continued to treat her.

But she had to at least try.

Her fingers trembled even more than before as she recommenced unfastening the buttons down the bodice of her gown, causing her to fumble several times before the last button was finally unfastened.

She hesitated, holding the two sides of her gown together, as she forced herself to look across at Hawksmere. 'Please attempt to hold your derision and scorn at bay, if only for a few minutes, if you please, Hawksmere.' Her voice shook with emotion.

Zachary frowned as he looked across at her searchingly, having no idea what it was that Georgianna was hiding from him. He was nevertheless aware that, whatever it was, it affected her deeply. 'Show me,' he encouraged gruffly, shoulders tensed.

Georgianna kept her eyes closed, her lips clamped firmly together, as she slowly parted the two sides of her gown before her fingers pulled down the soft material of her camisole, fully exposing her breasts to him.

It was impossible for Zachary to hold back his sharply indrawn breath as he saw the discoloured and livid scar between the swell of Georgianna's breasts for the first time.

Even from across the room he could see that the redness of the puckered and scarred skin now exposed to him was recent and several inches around. It was the same type of wound and scarring he had unfortunately seen many times during his years of battle against Napoleon's armies.

His gaze moved sharply back up to the pallor of Georgianna's face. Her eyes were once again open as she looked back at him with a flat and unemotional expression. He moistened lips that had gone suddenly dry.

'Is that...?'

'The result of a bullet wound?' Georgianna finished dully. 'Yes, it is.'

Zachary stood up, too restless, too disturbed by what he was seeing to remain seated for a moment longer. He crossed the room in long strides before gently pushing her fingers out of the way so that he might better see the livid red scar. 'How is it you did not die from such a wound?'

She gave an emotionally choked laugh. 'As it was so obviously intended that I should?'

'Yes.'

'How typical of you, Hawksmere, to cut straight to the point.' She looked up at him coldly. 'It was pure chance that I did not die, that the force of the bullet was deflected slightly by the locket I wore about my neck at the time.'

Zachary gave a dazed shake of his head, unable to stop looking at the terrible scarring that had been inflicted on Georgianna's otherwise beautiful and flawless skin. He was unable to stop himself from imagining a bullet entering Georgianna's smoothly perfect flesh, and the agony she must have suffered as it ripped through that delicate tissue, no doubt taking her down. Miraculously the locket prevented it from actually killing her.

He looked up, eyes narrowed. 'Who did this to you?'

Her smile turned humourless. 'Ah, and now comes the intelligence beneath the scorn and derision.'

'Georgianna.'

'Have you seen enough that I might refasten my gown now?' she challenged tensely.

His jaw clenched tightly as he demanded again, 'Who did this to you?'

Her eyes hardened to glittering violet jewels. 'Who do you imagine did it to me?' She refastened her gown without waiting for his permission. 'Who was it that you yourself said could not allow me to live once I had left him?'

'Rousseau,' he breathed softly.

'Exactly. Rousseau,' she confirmed flatly. 'Have you seen enough yet to believe me, Hawksmere?' she challenged tautly. 'Or would another scar help to finally convince you that everything I have told you is the truth?' She lifted a hand to move back the cluster of curls gathered on her left temple, revealing a long scar where a second bullet appeared to have grazed and broken her skin without actually penetrating it. 'This one was to be the coup de grâce, I believe. Unfortunately for André it was dark that night and I must have turned my head away at the last moment, because the second bullet only succeeded in rendering me unconscious rather than killing me outright.'

A single bullet to the heart and another to the head.

'An assassin's method,' Zachary acknowledged gruffly.

'Because André killed me,' Georgianna confirmed emotionally. 'Or, at least, he believed that he had when he left me for dead in that deserted forest just outside Paris,' she continued flatly. 'Which is where Monsieur Bernard, having heard the two shots and fearing for his livestock, found me unconscious and took me back to his farm.'

'The doctor?'

'The Bernards dare not call in a doctor, because they had no way of knowing who had inflicted such injuries. And, being unconscious, I could not tell them, either.' She smiled ruefully. 'Madame Bernard removed the bullet herself, then she sewed the wound back up as best she could. It could have been worse, I suppose, and *monsieur* might have lived alone and so been the one to attempt to sew the wound.'

'For pity's sake, be silent a moment, Georgianna.' Zachary choked as he finally found the breath to speak.

'Why?' she challenged. 'Did I not tell you yesterday that we all carry scars, some more visibly than others? Or does it sicken you to see such imperfection? It sickened me at the time. Although, in truth, I did not see the scars for some weeks,' she continued conversationally. 'I remained unconscious for several days afterwards and delirious for the better part of a week or more,' she explained flatly as Zachary looked at her sharply. 'And then, finally, when I did awaken it was to discover that I was blind, Zachary. Completely and utterly blind.' She raised her chin as she looked at him in defiant challenge.

'Dear God.'

'Yes.'

Zachary closed his eyes momentarily. 'That is the reason you do not like full dark.' It was a statement rather than a question.

'Yes. The blindness lasted only a couple of weeks, but it was the longest fortnight of my life, as I lay there wondering if I should ever see again. Do you believe me yet, Zachary?' she continued tauntingly. 'Or do you require further proof? If so, I am afraid I have none.'

'Stop it, Georgianna. For pity's sake.'

'Pity?' she echoed bitterly. 'And why should I pity you, Hawksmere? You were not the stupid fool who believed she was eloping with the man she believed herself in love with and whom she believed loved her, only to discover that she had been nothing more to him than a useful pawn. A pawn who was totally dispensable once he was safely returned to his native France and fellow conspirators.'

Zachary gave a dazed shake of his head. 'I meant only that you have had months to grow accustomed to this, Georgianna. I have had only a few minutes. Rousseau truly believes he has succeeded in assassinating you?'

'Oh, yes.'

'That is why you did not fear his looking for you after you had left him? Because he believed you already dead?'

She nodded abruptly. 'And my body then eaten by scavenging animals, yes.'

Now Zachary did feel sickened. But not by Georgianna's scars. Never that.

How could he ever be sickened by those, when they were the scars of the war she had been forced to fight alone, and in a country not her own? Indeed, it was the same evidence of war which he carried upon his own throat.

Georgianna might well have died, but for the kindness of a French farmer and his wife. And she had then placed herself in danger by working in a French tavern for months, followed by days of fearing being discovered at any moment as she waited at the dockside to return to England, so that she might bring back the information she had overheard of Napoleon's intention of leaving Elba.

There had been no father to defend her.

No brother to cherish her.

No husband to protect her.

Chapter Nine

'I demand to know where you are taking me,' Georgianna insisted even as she accepted Hawksmere's hand to aid her in climbing inside the ducal carriage.

Hawksmere waited until she was seated before climbing in behind her and sitting on the seat opposite as the door was closed. His expression was as grimly forbidding as it had been this past hour, since he had informed her she would be leaving Hawksmere House at the same time as he. 'Somewhere you will be safe.' He turned away to look out of the carriage window as it moved forward.

Georgianna had no idea what to expect from Hawksmere after her revelations to him earlier in the bedchamber. She had waited nervously as he went exceedingly quiet, restlessly pacing the room, so deep in thought he seemed almost to have forgotten she was there. Zachary had then come to an abrupt halt and instructed her to repack her bag and be ready to leave within the hour, before he had then departed her bedchamber.

There had been very little for Georgianna to re-pack. The things she had originally taken with her to France had all, apart from what she had carried in her reticule, been left behind when André took her to the forest outside Paris with the intention of killing her.

The Bernards had later provided her with a couple of worn gowns left behind by their daughter when she went off to marry her French soldier. And Georgianna had added two more gowns to that meagre wardrobe with the wages she'd earned at the tavern. She was wearing one of the only two sets of under-garments she possessed. As she had last night worn one of her only two nightgowns. Otherwise she had no other possessions.

Consequently she had spent most of that hour sitting in a chair beside the window, worrying about what Hawksmere intended to do with her now. As his final words had implied, he intended doing something.

'Is there such a place?' she prompted softly now.

Zachary turned back to look at her, his expression unreadable beneath the brim of his beaver hat as he answered her. 'I believe so, yes.'

Georgianna gave a pained frown. 'Is it your intention to foist me off on to one or other of your close friends? Perhaps that was the reason for Wolfing-ham's visit to you this morning?' she asked heavily.

Zachary now had cause to regret many things in his life. The nature of his marriage proposal to Georgianna Lancaster certainly being one of them. But the cruelty of his distrust of her these past two days, in light of the things she had revealed to him this morning, the terrible scars he had seen upon her body, and no doubt a reflection of the scars she also carried inside her, by far and away exceeded any previous regrets.

And Georgianna was as yet unaware of the worst of the cruelties of which he was guilty.

Once she did know then her disgust with him, her hatred of him, would no doubt be complete.

Zachary had consulted with no one on the decision, the change of plans, he had made in regards to what he should do with Georgianna when he left for France. He took full responsibility for that decision. And he challenged anyone to question him on it. If they dared.

As far as he was concerned, Georgianna had suffered enough. For her *naïveté* in regard to love, for her youthful belief and trust in a man who had used her and then attempted to kill her. Damn it, as far as Rousseau was concerned, he had killed her.

As Zachary now wished to kill Rousseau.

His hands clenched on his thighs with the need he felt to encircle the other man's throat and squeeze until no more air could enter Rousseau's lungs. To make him suffer, as Georgianna had surely suffered. First, by her humiliation in the man's duplicity. Then by being shot and left for dead. Regaining consciousness days later, only to find she was blind and in terrible pain. And then the months spent in Paris after that, and still fearing for her life. The latter because of her loyalty to England. A loyalty Zachary had distrusted and mocked her for, again to the point of cruelty.

Zachary was heartily ashamed of his harsh behaviour towards Georgianna these past two days. For having disbelieved her. For taunting her. And for then having made love to her, as if she were no better than that whore she had earlier denied being.

He could only try to make amends for those wrongs and hope that Georgianna might one day be able to forgive him.

And Rousseau deserved to die for his treatment of her.

Zachary intended seeing that it happened. Before too many days had passed, if he had his way. And he would. Because, in his eyes, Rousseau was no more than a rabid dog in need of being put down. Not for his loyalty to Napoleon, but for using an innocent, such as Georgianna had once been, to achieve his ends. For attempting and believing he had killed her when she was of no further use to him.

None of which helped to ease the burden of what Zachary now had to reveal to Georgianna, before then watching the hatred and contempt that would burn in those beautiful violet-coloured eyes towards him.

He drew in a long, controlling breath. 'I am taking you to your brother at Malvern House.'

Georgianna sat forward with a start, her face paling beneath her black bonnet. 'You cannot.' Her eyes were wide in her distress. 'Zachary, how can you be so cruel as to humiliate me further, by having my own brother turn away from me? I told you the truth earlier. I showed you.'

'There will be no humiliation, Georgianna.' Zachary sat forward on his own seat to reach out and grasp both of her tiny gloved hands in his, knowing it was possibly the last time she would allow him such familiarity. 'There will be no humiliation for you, Georgianna, and your brother will not turn away from you,' he assured evenly, 'because there was no scandal.'

She stilled at the same time as she blinked rapidly to hold back the tears now glistening in her eyes. 'I do not understand,' she finally murmured huskily.

And Zachary had no wish to tell her when he knew it would result in those beautiful eyes hardening with hatred for him. But his behaviour towards Georgianna this past two days allowed for no mercy being given on his own behalf. He deserved no forgiveness from her, no mercy. For any of the things he had said and done to her.

He released her hands to sit back against his seat as he looked across at her between narrowed lids. 'The notification of the ending of our betrothal appeared in the newspapers only a week after it was announced.'

Guilt coloured her cheeks. 'I expected no other.'

'That announcement stated,' Zachary continued firmly, 'that Lady Georgianna Rose Lancaster had decided, after all, against marrying Zachary Richard Edward Black, the Duke of Hawksmere.'

'But that is not what happened!'

'It also stated that it was your intention to retire to

the Malvern country estate for the remainder of the Season,' Zachary completed determinedly.

Georgianna now looked at him with wide, disbelieving eyes.

'Your father died in a riding accident only a month later,' Zachary continued evenly, 'at which time it was decided between your brother Jeffrey and myself that he would announce that you both intended to remain secluded at Malvern Hall for your time of mourning.'

She swallowed. 'What are you saying?'

Zachary drew in a deep breath before answering softly. 'That there was no scandal. As is acceptable, you were the one to end our betrothal and since then it is believed you have been living quietly at Malvern Hall with your brother.'

'How can this be?' Georgianna gave a dazed shake of her head.

The duke moved restlessly. 'Your father, brother and I discussed it after it was discovered you had eloped with Duval, or Rousseau, as he was later discovered to be. It was your family's hope that you would be found and returned before—well, before any harm might be done to your reputation and without any but the close family, and myself, being the wiser for it.'

Georgianna's cheeks became even more flushed in acknowledgement of the harm to which Hawksmere referred. 'And you agreed with this decision?'

Hawksmere's mouth tightened. 'Yes.'

'Because such an announcement lessened your own humiliation?'

His mouth thinned. 'No doubt that was part of it,' he allowed drily. 'But I hope I also thought of you, and your family, in that decision. I am not a vindictive man, Georgianna,' he assured evenly as she now looked at him blankly. 'No matter the impression I may have given to the contrary these past two days,' he acknowledged heavily.

Georgianna did not believe Hawksmere's behaviour to have been particularly vindictive towards her. She knew that she had fully deserved his anger, for her having eloped with another man so soon after the announcement of their own betrothal, causing him embarrassment. As she also deserved the distrust Zachary felt in regard to her return, when he knew that the man she had eloped with was actually a spy for Napoleon.

But this? Having allowed her to continue to think, these past two days, that she was unforgiven by her father and a pariah to her brother, the only family she had left in the world, as well as ostracised in society, was another matter entirely.

She frowned. 'Does no one in society know of my elopement with André?'

Hawksmere shrugged. 'A few may have guessed at the truth of the matter, but none knows for certain.'

'Then I am not shamed? Or ostracised?'

'No.'

'And does my brother know I shall be returning to him today?'

'I sent him a note earlier informing him so and

have received confirmation back from him, yes,' Hawksmere added softly.

'And does he welcome me back, despite knowing of my past behaviour?'

'He holds Rousseau completely responsible for past events.'

'Then I may return to my brother, my home, into society, without fear of rejection?'

A nerve pulsed in the tightness of Hawksmere's jaw. 'Yes.'

'And you have known this since we met again yesterday, known how much it pains me to think of my father's disappointment in me, to be estranged from Jeffrey? And yet you have continued to let me believe...' Georgianna did not even take the time to consider her next action, merely reacted, eyes glittering angrily as she lifted her hand and stuck Hawksmere across one hard and arrogant cheek.

Zachary had seen the angry spark in Georgianna's eyes, had noted the lifting of her gloved hand and guessed her intent. He'd made no attempt to avoid the painful slap she administered to the side of his face. Knowing he deserved it. That he deserved so much more than a single slap.

So, yes, let Georgianna slap him. Again and again, if that was her wish. Zachary would neither protest nor attempt to stop her.

'You are truly despicable!' Georgianna now glared across the width of the carriage at him. 'A despicable, unprincipled bastard! Oh, yes, Hawksmere,' she declared scornfully as he raised surprised dark brows.

'I assure you, I heard far worse than that during my months of working in Helene Rousseau's tavern. And you—you deserve to hear every one of those words for the way in which you have deceived me.' She blinked back the tears as they now blurred her vision of the arrogantly superior face across from her own.

'Perhaps we should take them as having already been said?' Zachary excused himself gruffly.

She gave an impatient shake of her head, her hands clenched together. 'I have spent months in despair of ever being able to see or speak to my brother again. Of ever seeing my home again. Of knowing that all in English society shunned me. This past few days of believing I would never be able to visit my father's graveside and beg his forgiveness. A despair which you might have spared me, if you had a mind to do so. If you had a heart with which to do so. Which you so obviously do not,' she added coldly.

Zachary had no defence against Georgianna's accusations. He knew he was guilty of everything she now accused him of. Except perhaps the latter.

It was true he had offered for Lady Georgianna Lancaster ten months ago because he needed a wife and an heir before his thirty-fifth birthday. It was true also that he had been more annoyed than concerned at the inconvenience when she had eloped with another man. As he had no doubt also agreed with Malvern's solution to that problem, as a way of saving himself deeper humiliation, as much as he had Georgianna's reputation.

But he had not really known Georgianna at that

time. Had seen only that plump pigeon, whom he'd decided would make him a suitable and undemanding wife, and a mother for his heirs.

The Georgianna with whom he had spent so many hours these past two days was not only a beautiful woman, but one for whom he knew he had felt a grudging admiration even before she had revealed the extent of the scars she bore, as evidence of Rousseau's betrayal of her.

She was also a woman for whom Zachary felt desire every time he so much as looked at her.

Even now, with her looking across at him with such contempt, Zachary was aware that his body pulsed with that same desire beneath his pantaloons.

Perhaps not as proof that he did indeed possess a heart, but enough so that Zachary knew he felt regret for the wide chasm that now yawned between the two of them. Fuelled by the dislike and contempt Georgianna now felt towards him.

His expression was grim as he nodded abruptly. 'I deserve each and every one of your accusations.'

She eyed him scathingly. 'That was never in any doubt.'

'No.'

Georgianna frowned her frustration with the calmness of Hawksmere's acceptance of her anger. What she really wanted was for him to mock or taunt her, as he usually did, so that she might have the satisfaction of slapping him again.

At the same time she felt as if a heavy weight had been lifted from her shoulders. She could see her

brother Jeffrey again. Could go to Malvern Hall and
visit her father's graveside and offer him her apologies
for her behaviour the previous year. Could return to
Malvern House if she wished. Take part in the upcoming Season, too, if that was what she decided to do.

Not that she intended telling Hawksmere of any of
the lightness and elation she felt; his contemptuous
behaviour towards her this past two days did not deserve to be forgiven, or forgotten, so easily.

At the same time as Georgianna knew she could
never forget his lovemaking of earlier this morning.

Having believed her to have been André's mistress
for several weeks, at least, Georgianna might have
expected Zachary to show contempt for her during
their lovemaking. Instead he had been poetical in his
appreciation of her body. Giving, even gentle, in his
caresses, as he introduced her to a pleasure she had
never imagined, let alone experienced.

But beneath all of that appreciation and gentleness
Zachary had been keeping the secret that she was not
in disgrace, after all, Georgianna reminded herself,
impatient with the softening of her emotions towards
him. Which surely must make him every inch that
bastard she had just called him?

'Again, I owe you my heartfelt apologies, Georgianna.'

She looked sharply across at him, unsure what he
was apologising for. For not telling her before now
that she was not in disgrace in society? Or for the intimacies of this morning?

Zachary sighed heavily as Georgianna made no

response to his apology. 'Except, of course, I do not possess a heart,' he acknowledged evenly. 'In which case, I will instead offer you my sincerest apologies. For having wronged you and hurt you these past two days.'

Deliberately. And without remorse. Each word was like the lash of the whip across the flesh on his back.

Georgianna looked across at him uncertainly. 'And is that supposed to excuse your behaviour?'

'No,' Zachary answered heavily.

'To make you feel better, perhaps?' she added scornfully.

He gave a humourless smile. 'If it was, then I assure you it has failed miserably.'

She raised haughty brows. 'I trust you will understand when I say that I am glad of that?'

How could he have ever thought this young woman was just a plump and malleable pigeon to be taken to the altar, impregnated, and then left forgotten and languishing on one of his country estates?

Even without her terrible experiences of this past year, he very much doubted that Georgianna would ever have been that malleable wife he had deliberately sought, and expected. If he had taken the time and trouble to get to know her, then he would have realised she possessed far too much spirit, was too emotional, to have ever settled for just being his ignored duchess and the mother of his heirs.

A spirit that was now denied him for ever.

Georgianna, quite rightly, would never forgive him for having deceived her. For deliberately allowing her to think she was still in disgrace. For imprisoning her. For making love to her.

'I understand, and completely accept, the anger you feel towards me.' He nodded abruptly just as the carriage drew to a halt outside Malvern House. 'Would you like me to come in with you or would you prefer to reconcile with your brother alone?'

Georgianna felt extremely nervous now that they had actually arrived at Malvern House, the same house she had always lived in whilst in London. The house where her brother Jeffrey now awaited her.

Her brother would be nineteen now and already he had been the Earl of Malvern this past nine months. Without benefit of even his sister to support him, with only that guardian, an elderly friend of her father's, to guide and help him.

'Georgianna!'

She was given no more time for those regrets, or the insecurity of wondering if Jeffrey really would be pleased by her return, as the carriage door was flung open and her brother himself hurtled inside the carriage before pulling her into his arms.

Georgianna gave a sob as she clung to Jeffrey, totally overwhelmed by the eagerness of his greeting, and being with someone she loved and who obviously still loved her. It had been so long since anyone had held her so tenderly, so unconditionally. Hawksmere's lovemaking did not count when she knew his motive had been revenge for her past misdemeanours towards her.

Zachary felt the unaccustomed sting of tears in his

own eyes as he witnessed the emotional reunion between brother and sister. Jeffrey with his usual youthful enthusiasm, Georgianna crying with joy as she clung to the younger brother she obviously adored and had missed so much.

A reunion that Zachary could have allowed her much sooner than this, if he'd had a mind to do so.

Georgianna might never forgive him for that, but Zachary knew he would never forgive himself, either. Or for any of his behaviour towards her these past two days.

Behaviour for which he would happily have got down on his knees and begged for forgiveness if he had thought it would do any good!

He raised a hand to the cheek that still stung from where Georgianna had slapped him just minutes ago. A vehemently delivered slap he had fully deserved.

As he deserved the tearfully accusing gaze she now gave him over her brother's shoulder.

Jeffrey was the one to finally pull back as he continued to beam down at his sister. Their colouring was similar, both were dark haired and blue eyed. 'Perhaps we should take this reunion into the house? Join us, Hawksmere?' Jeffrey prompted lightly as he glanced at Zachary.

Zachary saw the flash of resentment in Georgianna's eyes as she remained tucked beneath her brother's protective arm. 'I think not, thank you, Jeffrey. I have several other things in need of my attention this morning.' He excused himself.

The younger man frowned his disappointment. 'I thought you might at least come in for a few minutes?'

Zachary bit back his impatience. 'As I said, I have other things to do today.'

'I am sure we have taken up enough of Hawksmere's valuable time, Jeffrey,' Georgianna exclaimed without so much as a glance in the duke's direction.

'I did not think.' Jeffrey grimaced. 'Of course you are busy. But perhaps you would like to join us for dinner later this evening?'

'Jeffrey.'

'That will not be possible, I am afraid,' Hawksmere drawled over Georgianna's alarmed protest.

She blinked. 'His Grace is leaving.'

'For my country estate later today.' Once again the duke rudely spoke over Georgianna, his eyes flashing a reproving silver as he gave her a pointed glare. Evidence that Jeffrey was not one of the people privileged to know of Hawksmere's activities for the Crown.

Georgianna felt the warmth of that rebuke in her cheeks as she lowered her gaze. 'Of course.'

'Thank you for returning my sister to me.' Jeffrey grinned his pleasure at the older man as he held Georgianna close to his side.

Hawksmere nodded abruptly. 'I believe you will find that it was Georgianna who has returned herself to us all.'

She looked up at him sharply, searching that hard and arrogant face for some indication of Hawksmere's signature sarcasm and finding none. Instead he gazed across at her guardedly, as if unwilling to reveal his emotions. Which, no doubt, he was.

She straightened before speaking formally. 'I trust you will have a safe journey, your Grace.'

'As do I,' he drawled before turning to Jeffrey. 'I will be in touch when I return to town, Malvern.'

'We shall look forward to it, shall we not, Georgianna?' Jeffrey beamed enthusiastically.

'Of course,' Georgianna concurred softly, purposefully not looking at Hawksmere, knowing she would see only mockery for her there, both of them aware that if they never saw each other again it would be too soon for either of them.

And yet...

Once Georgianna had alighted from the carriage and begun slowly walking up the steps to Malvern House beside her brother, she was aware of a feeling of discomfort as she heard Hawksmere's carriage move on down the cobbled street. Of feeling slightly bereft at not knowing when, or if, she would see ever him again.

She was angry with him, yes, as her slap to his cheek had demonstrated. But what if he did not return from France? She was not angry enough, did not dislike him enough, to never wish to see him again.

Georgianna came to a halt on the top step into Malvern House before turning to gaze after Hawksmere's carriage, catching a brief glimpse of his profile inside the carriage as it turned the corner before disappearing from view.

'Are you well, Georgianna?'

She turned to find Jeffrey looking down at her with concern, his eyes bluer than her violet-coloured ones, his boyish face having grown handsome, chiselled, this past year. No doubt from his added responsibilities as Earl of Malvern. 'I am very happy to be home, thank you, Jeffrey,' she assured him warmly.

'You looked a little wistful for a moment. We shall see Hawksmere again very soon, I am sure,' he added reassuringly. 'He has become a regular visitor at Malvern House these past few months.'

'He has?' Georgianna looked up at her brother curiously as the two of them entered the house together, warmly accepting the butler's beam of pleasure and kind words at seeing her returned to Malvern House.

Jeffrey nodded. 'I have found his guidance invaluable these past months.'

'But what of your guardian? I would have thought that he would have been your mentor rather than Hawksmere?' Georgianna handed Carter her bonnet and gloves.

'Perhaps we should discuss this in the library,' Jeffrey requested before turning to the butler. 'Lady Georgianna and I would like hot chocolate and crumpets beside the fire, if you please, Carter.'

Georgianna's heart melted at the reminder of the way in which she and Jeffrey had passed many an afternoon together in the schoolroom when they were younger. 'Oh, yes, please, Carter.' She squeezed her brother's arm as they walked companionably to the library. 'It is so good to be back with you, Jeffrey,' she spoke emotionally once they were seated opposite each other beside the warmth of the fire.

Her brother sat forward, looking quite the dandy in his blue superfine and high-collared shirt. 'And you will tell me all about your adventures in a minute,' he promised. 'But first, did Hawksmere not talk to you of our guardian?'

'He mentioned that you have one,' Georgianna answered carefully, not sure of exactly what Zachary had told Jeffrey in his note in regard to when, how and why she had returned to England.

'We both have one, the same one, until we are both one and twenty,' Jeffrey corrected ruefully.

Georgianna's eyes widened. 'But…' She had a guardian? After all she had been through this past ten months, the independence, the decisions she had been forced to make for herself, she now had to suffer having a guardian until her birthday in three months' time? 'Who is it?' she demanded as a terrible foreboding began to wash over her.

Jeffrey grinned. 'Hawksmere, of course.'

That was the very answer Georgianna had begun to suspect, and dread.

Chapter Ten

'Would you care to tell me exactly what we are still doing in Paris, Zachary, when our mission was to sound out public feeling here, in regard to Napoleon's imminent arrival in Paris, before returning to England with our report?'

Zachary did not so much as glance at his companion as he kept his narrowed gaze levelled upon the establishment across the street from where the two of them stood, dressed as middle-class citizens of Paris.

'Do you remember Bully Harrison from Eton?'

There was a slight pause. 'How could I forget him, when he took such pleasure in beating the younger boys at every opportunity?' Wolfingham confirmed impatiently, green eyes hard. 'I also remember you taking an even greater delight in giving him a beating of your own, as a warning for him to instantly cease those unpleasant activities. Which he did. But I do not see what Harrison has to do with us being here in Paris.'

'There is an even worse bully inside that establishment.' Zachary nodded in the direction of the Fleur de Lis tavern across the street. 'A monster who took delight in hurting a woman.'

'Ah.'

'Indeed,' Zachary confirmed grimly.

'A woman of your acquaintance?'

'Yes.'

'Is she—? Did he hurt her very badly?'

Zachary's jaw tensed. 'He lied to her. Seduced her. For his own selfish reasons. And, when she was of no further use to him, he shot her. Twice. Once in the chest and then in the head.'

'Assassin!' Wolfingham hissed.

Zachary nodded. 'Miraculously she did not die. But she now lives in daily fear of the monster discovering his failure. Of him seeking her out and completing the assassination.'

Wolfingham glanced across at the tavern. 'And he is in there now?'

'I saw him enter a short time ago, with half-a-dozen cohorts.' Zachary nodded.

'Knife or pistol?'

'I believe I told you that he shot her.'

'I enquired as to whether you intend to use knife or pistol?'

Zachary's brow cleared slightly as he turned to look appreciatively at one of his closest friends. 'I apologise for underestimating you, Wolfingham,' he drawled ruefully. 'And I shall use my pistol. I believe I should like him to know what it is like to stare down the barrel of a gun and know you are about to breathe your last,' he added with grim satisfaction as he thought of how Georgianna must have suffered the night Rousseau attempted to kill her. And he wasn't just thinking of her physical wounds, but the emotional ones he doubted would ever completely heal.

There was little enough he could do to make amends for the emotional wounds he had inflicted on her since, but dispatching Rousseau was certainly a start.

'I should warn you, though, I have reason to believe the man may recognise me,' Zachary warned, unconsciously touching the definitive scar upon his throat.

Wolfingham nodded. 'What would you like me to do in order to divert his cohorts?'

Zachary gave a hard grin. 'Succinct and to the point—I have always liked that about you.'

'A man who would treat a woman in such a despicable way does not deserve to live.'

A sentiment exactly matched by Zachary's feelings on the matter.

Georgianna paced restlessly up and down the yellow salon at Malvern House, totally unaware of the luxuriously appointed room she had so enjoyed choosing the décor and furnishings for just two short years ago.

Those two years might just as well have been twenty.

Because she was not that same person who had

once so painstakingly pored over swatches of materials for curtains and furnishings for weeks on end, voicing a complaint when the material on one of the chairs proved to be the merest shade darker than its twin.

It all seemed so unimportant now, so petty. As had the ordering of the new gowns Jeffrey had insisted upon, in preparation for their return to society, when it was discovered that all of last year's gowns were far too big for her now-slender figure.

A society with its rules and strictures upon behaviour and speech, which she had so long believed she wished to be part of again, but now found totally stifling.

As she did the fact that those calls and entertainments continued, as if Napoleon and his ever-increasing army were not even now marching doggedly and triumphantly towards Paris.

Indeed, the majority of the *ton* seemed far more interested in the fact that Lady Georgianna Lancaster was returned to town, inciting an avalanche of calls and invitations from those of the *ton* who had already returned in preparation for the full Season.

Polite calls and invitations, which had nevertheless possessed an underlying curiosity to know as to how she had spent the past year. Georgianna had answered all of those queries with the same reply Jeffrey had given at the time of her disappearance; she had spent her time quietly at Malvern Hall, initially following the breaking of her betrothal, and then in mourning for the death of their father.

As Hawksmere had said, some might suspect otherwise, but none dared question the word of either the Duke of Hawksmere or the new Earl of Malvern.

Hawksmere.

As might be expected, there had been neither sight nor sound of Zachary Black and Georgianna could only presume, having heard nothing to the contrary, that silence must mean he was still in France. Perhaps he was even now witnessing Napoleon's triumphant march towards Paris.

If not, then he would no doubt have made a point of calling upon his two wards before now.

Georgianna had far from forgiven Hawksmere for that deception!

As no doubt Hawksmere, in his turn, did not believe he had any need to explain himself to anyone, least of all the two young people who were now under his guardianship.

Georgianna could only wonder what on earth had possessed her father to choose such a man as guardian to his young son and daughter, most especially when that daughter had eloped in order to escape marriage to that same gentleman.

Which was perhaps answer enough as to why Hawksmere had been chosen. As he already knew of the scandal behind the breaking of their betrothal, making him their guardian had meant there would be no need for Georgianna's absence to be explained to a third party after her father's death.

Which did not make the unpleasant fact of being under the guardianship of Hawksmere, of all men, for another three months, any more acceptable to Georgianna.

Something she intended informing him of at the earliest opportunity.

In the meantime, Georgianna was returned to her family, to her home. She already had a whole new wardrobe of gowns, deliberately designed to hide the unsightly scar upon her chest, in which she could receive guests, as well as drive out in the family carriage in the afternoons. She and Jeffrey had also spent some time in deciding which social invitations they could or should accept, when their year of mourning was not quite at an end.

And it all seemed so pointless to Georgianna. So uninspiring. So unexciting after her months of freedom from those strictures.

Oh, she could not deny that they had been terrifying, uncertain months, too. Days and nights when she had feared for her very life. Which was perhaps one of the reasons she was so restless and bored by the tedium of her life now?

And the other reason?

Again that was down to Hawksmere.

Angry as she was with him—furious, in fact— Georgianna could not deny that everything seemed so much duller, flatter, without Hawksmere's arrogantly powerful presence.

Which was utterly ridiculous on her part, when she should be relishing that dullness after so many months spent in fear and torment.

A fear and torment that was not over and never

could be whilst the danger of André Rousseau lurked so ominously in the shadows of her life.

'Is it time for hot chocolate and crumpets beside the fire again?'

Georgianna turned with a smile as her brother quickly crossed the room to kiss her warmly upon the cheek.

'What makes you say that?'

Jeffrey looked down at her quizzically. 'You looked very forlorn and wistful when I entered the room.'

Forlorn and wistful?

Because of her thoughts of Hawksmere?

No, of course it had not been because of thoughts of Hawksmere; she had been thinking of André, not Zachary, when Jeffrey entered the salon. 'I believe I am still adjusting to being back in England and society,' she excused lightly.

'But you are pleased to be, surely?' he cajoled.

Barely a year separated them in age and Jeffrey had certainly matured exponentially during his months as the Earl of Malvern under Hawksmere's guidance. But still Georgianna felt so much older than her brother now, in her emotions as well as her interests.

Not that she could explain to Jeffrey without fear of revealing too much of her experiences over the past year.

They had necessarily talked of her elopement, her parting from André, her months of working, though she had not revealed exactly where she had worked, only that it was in a kitchen, to earn the money for her boat passage back to England. Not once during their conversations had Georgianna told Jeffrey the complete truth about the months she had spent in France. How could she, when that truth was so horrible, so demeaning, so frightening?

It was a truth which only Hawksmere knew for certain.

Such was her brother's obvious admiration and liking for the older man, and oblivious of their guardian's work for the Crown, Jeffrey had so far not questioned why she had chosen to go to Hawksmere, of all people, immediately upon returning to England. Nor had Georgianna chosen to enlighten her brother as to the exact day of her return, or that she had been kept a prisoner in Hawksmere's home for two days and nights.

She might be angry with Zachary, resentful even, but it served no purpose for her to confide in her brother, when he obviously admired Hawksmere so. The older man was to be his guardian for some time to come. Also, it could endanger the work Zachary even now carried out for the Crown.

'Of course.' She gave her brother a brightly reassuring smile. 'I am merely finding it strange, after so many months away.'

'In that case, a dinner party is exactly what is required.' Her brother moved to the fireplace to warm his hands, the darkness of his hair appearing blue-black in the firelight.

'A dinner party?' Georgianna's pulse jumped in nervousness, her heart leaping in her chest, as she joined Jeffrey beside the fire. 'But I thought tomorrow evening at Lady Colchester's musical soirée was to be our first appearance back into society?' Individual calls by members of society was one thing, as was riding in her carriage in the afternoons, but Georgianna was dreading having that society staring at her *en masse* and wondering if any of the rumours that so abounded about her were true.

'I should have said a dinner party *en famille*,' Jeffrey corrected cheerfully. 'Hawksmere has sent word he is returned from the country and wishes the two of us to join him at Hawksmere House for dinner this evening.'

Hawksmere?

Georgianna moved to sit down abruptly on the chair beside the fireplace, her knees feeling suddenly weak at the knowledge that Zachary was returned from France. And safely, too, if he was inviting the two of them to join him for dinner this evening.

'You have seen him?' she prompted huskily.

'He sent for me this afternoon.' Jeffrey nodded.

But not her, Georgianna realised. Because she would be his ward for only a matter of months more? Or because he had no wish to see her again? Including her in this evening's dinner invitation was, after all, what Jeffrey would have expected of their guardian.

'Hawksmere is hardly family, Jeffrey,' she remonstrated stiffly.

'As good as,' he dismissed unconcernedly, seeming completely unaware of Georgianna's reaction to the news of Hawksmere's invitation.

Georgianna had not realised until that moment how worried she had been about Zachary's safe return from France.

A concern she was starting to fear might be based on something other than the anger she bore towards him, for once again having omitted to tell her the full truth.

'It really was not necessary for you to include me in this dinner invitation, Hawksmere!'

Zachary found himself smiling for the first time in days as Georgianna attacked him with her acerbic tongue the moment she entered the blue salon of his home on her brother's arm, rather than offering the expected polite greeting.

'And how gratified you must be to know that there is only the matter of three months before you will be relieved of my guardianship,' he continued haughtily even as she sketched him a polite curtsy.

'Georgianna?' Jeffrey looked nonplussed by his sister's sharpness towards their guardian.

Zachary, on the other hand, found himself highly entertained. 'The history between your sister and me necessarily means that we are still working on acquiring an acceptable politeness between the two of us, Jeffrey,' he excused to the younger man, even as he stepped forward to take Georgianna's gloved hand in his, his own gaze meeting her glittering violet one as he raised that hand to his lips. 'You are looking exceptionally lovely this evening, Georgianna,' he drawled as he straightened before slowly relinquishing her hand.

She did indeed look very beautiful, the darkness of her hair fashionably styled so as to conceal the scar at her temple. Her fashionable gown was the same violet colour as her eyes, with a swathe of lace artfully fashioned across the top of her bosom, so concealing the scar Zachary knew she also bore there.

'I am sure there is no need for false politeness between the two of us in the privacy of your home, Hawksmere,' she dismissed offhandedly as she moved away, at the same time reminding Zachary, at least, that he had not felt the need for this same politeness the last time she had been in his home. 'Jeffrey cannot help but be aware of the reason for our strained relationship.'

Zachary raised dark brows. 'I had hoped we had come to a different understanding of each other since your return?'

Those violet coloured eyes flashed darkly. 'Only in as much as I believe that we have come to an acceptance of our hearty dislike of each other.'

'Georgianna!'

'Do not be alarmed, Jeffrey.' Once again Zachary soothed his younger ward's shock at his sister's rudeness. 'Georgianna and I understand each other perfectly. Do we not, Georgianna?' The hardness of his tone was a warning for her to temper her anger and dislike of him. Her behaviour was not only alarming her brother, but also implied that they knew each other far better than their previously known acquaintance might imply.

Which they obviously did.

Zachary had thought of Georgianna often these past two weeks, whilst he was away in France. More often than he might have wished, if truth be known, and not just because of his dealings with Rousseau.

Georgianna had only been a prisoner in his home for a matter of thirty-six hours, but they had been intensely intimate hours. Hours, when Zachary came to know Georgianna rather better than he had ever known any woman. Hours, when he had come to admire her, for her spirit and determination. Hours, when he had come to like, even appreciate, her outspokenness and the way that she refused to be cowed by anything he did or said to her. Hours, when he had come to desire her more than any woman of his acquaintance.

As he desired her still, Zachary acknowledged as he studied her through narrowed lids.

Georgianna appeared less strained than she had been two weeks ago, the lines smoothed from her forehead and beside her eyes and mouth, and there was a becoming colour in the smoothness of her cheeks and full, pouting lips. But she still looked too slender in that violet-coloured gown. Perhaps more so, her unadorned neck and throat appearing delicately vulnerable, as did the slenderness of her arms.

And Zachary's desire to possess all that loveliness was almost painful.

Damn it, it was painful.

His body throbbed with desire for her even more after their two weeks apart.

'Yes, Hawksmere, I believe we do indeed understand each other. Perfectly.' She lifted her chin in challenge.

Zachary very much doubted that Georgianna's understanding of that statement was the same as his own. Because, without the strictures Jeffrey's presence necessarily put on his behaviour, Zachary very much doubted he would be able to control the desire he now felt to make love to Georgianna again.

And not just physically. He ached to possess all of her. Her spirit. Determination. Her outspokenness. Along with her often sarcastic sense of humour, the latter more often than not at his own expense.

Georgianna had shown him this evening, with just a few brief words, that she disliked him as much now as she ever had.

Which was no doubt a fitting punishment for his having proposed marriage to her so shabbily the previous year. And Zachary knew he had again treated her abominably when she returned from France so unexpectedly.

Was it any wonder that she now disliked him so intensely?

Or that he, having thought about her so much, remembering over and over again making love to her, touching her, kissing her, bringing her to completion, desired her more now than he had two weeks ago?

'Are you ill, Hawksmere?' she now taunted mockingly. 'You have gone exceedingly quiet for someone who I believed always had an answer for everything.'

'I say, Georgianna…' cautioned Jeffrey.

Zachary held his hand up to prevent Jeffrey from continuing to chastise his sister on his behalf. 'I do not believe I as yet have the answer to you, dearest Georgianna,' he assured softly.

Georgianna felt the burn of colour in her cheeks, knowing she had brought Hawksmere's taunt upon herself by her challenging and rude behaviour. Except she could not seem to behave in any other way when in his company, her hackles rising, defences instantly up, as she verbally attacked him. Before she was attacked herself?

Maybe so, but she certainly did not appreciate his sarcasm in addressing her as 'dearest Georgianna', when they both knew she was here on sufferance only. Because it would have appeared odd to Jeffrey if his sister had not been included in the dinner invitation from their guardian. A guardianship, in regard to herself, that Georgianna had no doubt Zachary found tiresome, to say the least.

'It is a woman's prerogative to remain something of a mystery to a gentleman, is it not?' she dismissed airily, very aware that this man knew her far better than any other, physically as well as emotionally.

Challenging Zachary the moment the two of them met again had been Georgianna's only way of dealing with those memories of their previous intimacy, her only defence against the rush of emotions and the memories, which had threatened to overwhelm her the moment she looked at him. Of him kissing her, caressing her, pleasuring her, with those sculptured lips and large, and wholly seductive, hands!

There was no denying that Zachary looked very handsome this evening, in his black evening clothes and snowy white linen. His hair had grown longer this past two weeks and now curled silkily about his ears and nape. He appeared slightly thinner in the face, too, no doubt from the weeks he had spent in the turmoil of France, bringing into stark relief his handsome features.

Just to look at him caused Georgianna's heart to beat faster and the palms of her hands to dampen inside her lace gloves.

'So it is,' he drawled in answer to her comment as Hinds appeared discreetly in the doorway. 'Shall we go into dinner now?' He offered Georgianna his arm.

Georgianna hesitated at the offered intimacy, having no desire to touch Zachary, to be made so totally aware of him, and of those memories that had haunted, and so bedevilled, her these past two weeks.

Nevertheless, she forced herself to show no emotion as she placed her gloved hand upon his arm and walked beside him to the dining room.

The same intimate dining room in which she and Zachary had dined alone together two weeks ago.

Chapter Eleven

'I'm sure you will have received many visitors and invitations now that you are returned to society?'

'Hawksmere, I give you permission to cease all attempts at this strained politeness between the two of us for the time my brother is out of the room,' Georgianna dismissed impatiently, Jeffrey having excused himself on a call of nature just a few short minutes ago.

Zachary smiled at her customary straightforwardness. Georgianna was right: their efforts at maintaining that imposed social politeness, because of Jeffrey's presence, had become more and more difficult as dinner progressed, to the point that even the boyishly enthusiastic Jeffrey had seemed to become uncomfortable in their company.

'I am far more interested in knowing how things progress in France than in the two of us being socially polite to each other,' Georgianna prompted interestedly as she sat forward eagerly.

Zachary gave a guarded shrug. 'As you say, they progress. At least, Napoleon does,' he added grimly.

She gave a soft gasp. 'And do you believe he will be successful in his endeavour?'

Zachary did not bother in so much as attempting to dismiss Georgianna's concerns. She was far too intelligent to be fobbed off. Besides which, the months she had spent in France had given her an insight into the turmoil which had once again beset that country. 'I do not believe I am breaking any confidences by revealing that his army grows bigger by the day and that he will soon enter Paris itself.'

'And the king?'

'I believe Louis is preparing to flee.'

Georgianna's cheeks grew pale. 'Then there will most certainly be another war.'

'Undoubtedly.'

She flicked him a glance beneath long silky dark lashes. 'You will be a part of that war?'

'Most certainly.' Zachary gave her a mocking grin. 'Just think, Georgianna, I might even manage to get myself killed, and in doing so relieve you of the burden of suffering both my guardianship as well as my company.'

Georgianna frowned across at him darkly. 'You are being unfair by inferring that I have ever wished you dead, Hawksmere.'

'Just consigned to Hades.'

'Well, yes, there is that.' A beguiling dimple appeared in her cheek as she smiled genuinely for what seemed to be the first time this evening. 'A little singeing by those hellish fires, at the very least, might succeed in stripping you of some of your irritating arrogance.'

Zachary found himself chuckling. 'I do believe I have missed both you and your insults, Georgianna.'

She raised dark brows. 'Somehow I doubt that very much!'

Then she would be wrong, Zachary acknowledged. Georgianna was a woman with whom he now spoke almost as freely, and on similar subjects, as he did his closest male friends. Something he had not believed possible with any woman in society.

It had long been his experience that the women of society preferred not to know of the more unpleasant facts of life, their main topics of conversation seeming to be fashions, gossip, and the managing of their household and family. Georgianna's experiences this past year had taken her far beyond being interested in such trivialities.

Reminding Zachary only too forcibly that there was something he needed, rather than wished, to discuss with her in private.

'You will not allow Jeffrey to fight?' Georgianna looked at him anxiously now.

Zachary frowned. 'He is a man grown, Georgianna.'

'And you are his guardian.' Her eyes glittered a deep, emotional violet.

'And, no doubt, you will never forgive me if something should happen to him.' It was a statement rather than a question.

'And I doubt my forgiveness is of the least interest, or importance, to you.'

'You might be surprised,' Zachary murmured softly before sighing as Georgianna continued to look at him expectantly. 'I make no promises, but I will see what can be done to prevent Jeffrey from rushing headlong into the coming war,' he added grimly.

She sighed. 'He admires you tremendously, you know.'

'Unlike his sister,' Zachary drawled drily.

She gave him a brief glance. 'It is not a question of not admiring you, Hawksmere. Indeed, I admire your endeavours on behalf of the Crown enormously.'

'That is something, I suppose,' he drawled.

'The rest of your personality leaves a lot to be desired, of course,' she added caustically, 'but one cannot have everything.'

'As usual, the sword thrust in the velvet glove.'

Georgianna eyed him mockingly. 'At least I am consistent.'

'Oh, you are most certainly that, Georgianna,' Zachary allowed before sobering. 'Is it convenient for you to come here tomorrow afternoon?'

'Why?' She eyed him warily now.

He grimaced. 'I would prefer to discuss that with you tomorrow.'

And Georgianna would prefer to know now what that discussion was to be about.

Unfortunately, Jeffrey chose that moment to return to the dining room, so putting an end to their own conversation as they all began to talk instead of the invitations they had accepted for the coming season.

'Thank you, Hinds.' Georgianna smiled politely at the butler as he showed her into the blue salon of Hawksmere House the following afternoon.

After she had spent the night, and all of this morning, fretting and worrying as to what it was Hawksmere could possibly wish to discuss with her today in private.

Hawksmere himself had his back turned towards her as he stood in front of one of the large bay windows, looking out of into the garden beyond. He turned the moment the door closed as evidence of his butler's departure.

'I did not think, when I asked you to come here.' He frowned darkly. 'You do at least have a maid with you, I hope?'

Georgianna nodded. 'She is waiting out in the hallway.'

'Would you care for refreshment?' the duke offered politely. 'Tea, perhaps?'

She eyed him scathingly. 'The only time I have been in this house, apart from that surreal dinner with Jeffrey yesterday evening, was as your prisoner, so, no, I do not require the nicety of tea, thank you, Hawksmere.'

'The time for social politeness between the two of us really is over then, hmm?' he guessed drily.

'I am not sure it ever began.'

Once again Zachary found himself chuckling at

Georgianna's honesty. 'Let us at least sit down,' he invited ruefully.

'You consider I might feel a need to do so, once you have spoken with me?' she murmured concernedly as she moved to perch demurely on the edge of one of the armchairs.

Zachary had debated with himself long and hard as to what he should tell Georgianna about Rousseau. And still he had no real answer, only knew that she needed to know that the other man no longer posed a threat, to her liberty or her life.

She looked so lovely today, dressed in a gown of pale silver, the darkness of her curls peeping out from beneath the matching bonnet, her face youthfully flushed by the freshness of the breeze outside, that Zachary baulked at even introducing the subject of her previous lover.

Her previous lover?

Well, yes, because the intimacies the two of them had shared two weeks ago meant that Zachary had certainly been Georgianna's most recent lover.

And now that he was alone with her once again, he found that the last thing he wished to do was talk of Rousseau.

'Have you thought of me at all this past two weeks, Georgianna?' he found himself prompting huskily.

She blinked at the unexpectedness of his question. 'Politely or impolitely?'

'Oh, impolitely, I am sure,' he allowed with another laugh.

'Then, yes, I do believe I have thought about you. Often,' she added pointedly.

Zachary smiled ruefully. 'And were all these impolite thoughts unpleasant ones?'

Georgianna was uncertain where Zachary was going with this line of questioning. They were two people who had once been betrothed to each other and now found themselves thrust into a situation not of their choosing. She very much doubted that Zachary had wished to become her guardian, any more than she now wished him to be. And that was without the awkwardness of the intimacies which had taken place between the two of them two weeks ago. That certainly made for a very strained relationship between the two of them.

To a degree that Georgianna had found herself wondering many times since how such a thing could ever have happened between two people who could not even claim a liking for each other?

And then she remembered the touch of Zachary's hands upon her, his lips, his tongue, and she knew exactly how such a thing had occurred between them. They were a man and a woman, who had been forced into a situation of close proximity. Factor in Zachary's feelings of anger towards her for past wrongs, then making love to her, ensuring that she enjoyed having him make love to her, and those intimacies had become inevitable.

Her own response to them she found harder to explain.

'Unpleasant enough,' she answered him sharply as she stood up restlessly. 'Now…?'

'I thought of you, too, whilst I was away, Georgianna.'

She stilled, once again eyeing him warily. 'Oh, yes?'

Zachary nodded, his expression intense. 'They were not unpleasant thoughts at all.'

Georgianna's heart began to beat loudly in her chest, her cheeks suddenly warm. 'You surprise me.'

'Do I?' He crossed the room silently until he stood only inches away, looking down at her. 'Does it really surprise you that I remember our time together here so vividly and so pleasantly, Georgianna?' he repeated huskily.

It did, yes. Hawksmere had not earned his reputation, as one of the five Dangerous Dukes, solely on his war record. No, his exploits in the bedchamber were also lauded by the ladies of England and much envied by the gentlemen. Georgianna did not imagine that someone as inexperienced as herself would have been in the least memorable amongst the dozens of beauties who were reputed to have shared a bed with Hawksmere.

As she had done. However briefly.

Her legs trembled slightly, hands clasped tightly together, as she looked up at him. 'It would surprise me very much,' she answered stiltedly.

'And yet?'

'I really would rather not talk about that particular subject, Hawksmere.' She had meant the words to come out as a set-down, but instead they sounded wistful and yearning.

Yearning?

Could it be that she secretly wanted there to be a repeat of the events, the intimacies, they had shared that morning in the bedchamber above them?

That would be madness on her part.

Georgianna's thoughts were broken off abruptly, indeed, her mind went a complete blank, as Zachary took her in his arms and claimed her lips firmly with his own.

The passion and desire were instantaneous, as Zachary's arms tightened about her even as his mouth devoured hers hungrily. It was all that Georgianna could do to remain on her feet, by clutching tightly to the tops of his muscled arms as she returned the heat of those kisses.

Zachary broke the kiss to graze his lips against the softness of Georgianna's cheek. 'I have thought this past two weeks—' he kissed her earlobe '—of doing this again.' He tasted the delicate column of her neck. 'Constantly.' His tongue sought out the hollows at the base of her throat, the creamy softness of the tops of her breasts through the silver lace. 'And none of those thoughts matched up to this reality,' he acknowledged gruffly, his body throbbing and achingly engorged. 'God, how I want you, Georgianna!'

She gasped. 'Zachary, we cannot. We must not.'

'I must,' he rasped fiercely as he lifted her up in his arms and carried her over to the chaise. He lay her down on its softness and sat down beside her, his gaze holding hers as he untied her bonnet before removing it completely.

'You have the most beautiful hair, Georgianna, so soft and silky.' He removed the pins as he spoke, before gazing down at her appreciatively as he loosened those curls about her shoulders.

'Zachary,'

'And your skin is like the finest ivory.' His gaze followed the path of his hand as it trailed down the column of her throat to the swell of her breasts. 'So pale and so soft to the touch.' He pushed the lace aside to reveal the scar between her breasts. A scar Zachary did not find any more repellent than she appeared to find the one upon his own throat. No, he considered this scar to be Georgianna's own, very private, war wound.

A sign, a remembrance, of the battle she had fought, and won, and which now only he and she had knowledge of.

'You can have no idea how much I have thought of making love to you again, Georgianna,' he groaned achingly.

Georgianna thought, from the intensity of his kisses and the fire now gleaming, burning, in the silver depths of his eyes as he slowly lowered his head, that she might hazard a guess.

And the thought that this man, that Zachary, wanted her so deeply he had thought of her even whilst he was away in the turmoil of France, filled her with an elation, a happiness Georgianna had not even known she secretly longed for.

She gasped as she felt the warmth of his lips against the scar on her chest. 'Zachary, don't.'

'Let me, Georgianna.' He breathed hotly against her even as his lips continued to kiss every inch of that scarred flesh.

'It is unsightly.' It took every effort of will Georgianna possessed to stop herself from pulling that lace back over the disfiguring scar on her chest, her jaw tight, her hands clenched at her sides.

'No more so than my own scar. Does that repulse you?'

'How could it, when it is evidence of your bravery?' she assured unhesitatingly.

He looked up at her darkly. 'As your own scar is a part of the brave and beautiful woman that you are. One who has suffered and yet survived.'

'I barely survived, Zachary,' she reminded weakly.

'And you are all the braver and stronger for it.'

Was she braver and stronger? Stronger, certainly, but she did not think herself braver. She still suffered nightmares in her bed at night. Dreamt constantly of that night in the woods. The pain, both emotional and physical, that she had suffered. The terror of waking up blind and in so much pain. The months afterwards when she had continued to fear for her life.

Of still suffering from that same fear.

Georgianna's limbs turned to water, all other thoughts fleeing her mind, her hands moving up to entwine her fingers in the darkness of Zachary's hair as he unfastened the buttons at the front of her gown and she felt the warmth of his lips against the bare swell of her breast.

She cried out achingly as his lips parted and he took the aroused and aching tip of that breast into the heat of his mouth, before suckling, gently at first, and then more deeply, hungrily. She arched up into him, instinctively seeking, wanting more, receiving more as Zachary's hand cupped beneath her other breast and he began to roll and squeeze the second nipple to the same arousing rhythm.

The sensations were overwhelming. An all-consuming heat and a glorious pleasure that radiated out from her breasts and coursed through the rest of her body, her nipples both hard and aching, the folds between her thighs swelling and moistening, the muscles deep inside her contracting and squeezing hungrily.

And it was a selfish need.

'Zachary?' She breathed weakly as she felt his hand trailing along her calf, pushing up her gown to above her knees and then higher still, until she felt the warm brush of air against those heated and swollen folds between her thighs.

'Allow me to pleasure you again, Georgianna,' he groaned, his breath a hot caress against the dampness of her nipple. 'Grant me that, at least.'

'But what of your own pleasure?' She knew very little about men, but she knew enough to know that Zachary's erection was both hard and demanding as it pressed, pulsed, against her hip.

'I am happy in the knowledge that I please you, Georgianna.'

'No.'

'I am not pleasing you?' Zachary pulled back slightly, his expression one of concern. 'Did I hurt you? Was I too rough with you just now?'

Delicate colour warmed her cheeks. 'I did not say that.'

'Then what?'

'Zachary...' Her gaze could no longer meet his, aware as she was of the fact that the top of her gown still gaped open, revealing the fullness of her breasts. The bare fullness of her breasts. 'Pleasure is surely to be given as well as received?'

'Yes.'

Georgianna moistened stiff lips. 'Then of course I should like to give you pleasure, too. If you will teach me, show me, what pleases you,' she added uncomfortably, knowing that she was far less experienced, make that lacking in experience at all, than all those other women Zachary was reputed to have made love with.

Zachary looked down at her searchingly. It had been his experience in the past that there was no *of course* about it, when it came to a man's pleasure during lovemaking. Whores were one thing and would do what they were asked for with the giving of coin. Wives, he had heard, preferred the act to be without embellishment and over with as quickly as was possible for the begetting of an heir. Other women in society, those married women who took a lover once the heir and spare had been provided, usually considered it enough that they were giving carte blanche with their body and, as such, had no interest in what she might do to please the man in her bed.

Obviously Georgianna was different from all those other women, being neither whore, nor wife, nor a married woman in society looking for a lover. As he could only assume she also meant she wanted him to show her, to teach her, what best pleased him in particular, rather than...

No, he refused to think of Georgianna's relationship with Rousseau now. He would not allow anything or anyone else to intrude upon their stolen time together. 'Are you sure you wish to pleasure me, Georgianna?' he prompted huskily.

She flickered a glance up at him before looking down again.

'It seems only fair I should do so, after—after you gave to me so unselfishly when—when we were last together.' The colour flooded her cheeks once again.

'That did not answer my question.'

Because Georgianna had no idea how to answer his question! She knew nothing of lovemaking, be it man or woman. She only knew, from these times with Zachary, that she could not be a selfish lover, that she wished to please Zachary as he had pleased her. As her own achingly aroused body said she now must.

'What would you be willing to do to give me pleasure, Georgianna?' he prompted huskily at her silence.

'Whatever you wished me to do.'

'Anything?'

She swallowed at the intensity of his silver gaze fixed unblinkingly on her blushing face. 'I believe so, yes.'

He smiled ruefully. 'Words are easily spoken, Georgianna.'

'Then I shall answer in deeds rather than words.' She sat up before sliding down to the base of the chaise to swing her feet on to the floor, before standing up and turning to face Zachary.

His eyes widened in surprise as she put her hands on his shoulders and pushed him down on to his back on the chaise before sitting beside him; obviously Hawksmere was not a man used to a woman taking charge in the bedchamber. Or in this case, the blue salon of his London home.

Georgianna was not a woman used to taking charge in lovemaking, either, but in this case it seemed completely desirable.

Besides, she had not spent all of her time in the kitchen, or the storeroom, at Helene Rousseau's tavern. She had occasionally ventured out to help serve behind the bar if they were especially busy; some of the surprising acts she had witnessed between the male and female customers when she did so had made her blush to the roots of her hair. There had been one act in particular that the gentlemen had seemed to enjoy very much.

If Georgianna only had the courage to now put into practise all that she had witnessed.

'I believe I should like to kiss you as you once kissed me.' She licked her lips in anticipation.

'Georgianna?'

She glanced up enquiringly from where she had already unfastened the buttons on Zachary's pantaloons and was now in the process of untying his drawers. The bulge beneath the linen, stretching and tightening that material, was making that task more difficult than it ought to be and was certainly causing a lack of sexual prowess on her part.

'What are you doing?' He looked pained as she at last managed to unfasten his drawers and reached inside to withdraw the pulsing and throbbing hard length beneath.

Georgianna's fingers stilled as she looked down at him uncertainly. 'You do not like it?'

'Oh, I most assuredly do like it, Georgianna!' he breathed shakily. 'I am just— Are you sure you wish— Do you know what you are doing?'

Colour burned her cheeks. 'I am sure I shall not be as experienced as some of your other ladies, but…'

'That is not at all what I meant,' he grated from between gritted teeth, his fingers having curled about the slenderness of her wrists to halt her movements. 'And I have said there will be no talk between the two of us of any others. I merely wanted to know if you are sure this is what you want. What you would enjoy.'

She glanced down at the thick length of his arousal as she slowly curled her fingers about it, the skin feeling surprisingly soft as velvet.

Georgianna swiped her tongue over her lips. 'It

most certainly appears to be what a certain part of you wants,' she murmured with satisfaction at Zachary's obvious response to her touch.

Zachary could not deny that. Had no desire to deny it. Indeed, just seconds ago he had feared he might spill at the first touch of the softness of Georgianna's fingers closing about him.

He had managed to hold, thank goodness, but he could not deny that his instinct was still to thrust into those encircling fingers, to bid her grip him tighter, stroke him faster, harder, as they worked together towards his release.

'I merely want you to be sure—' Zachary broke off with a strangled groan of pleasure as Georgianna lowered her head, her long hair falling in a soft caress against his thighs as she licked the silken tip. A long and rasping lick that caused him to arch up off the chaise.

'You like that.' She repeated that slow and agonisingly pleasurable rasp.

Liked it? Zachary had thought of this woman constantly this past two weeks, had imagined time and time again making love to her again, pleasuring her again. And in none of those imaginings had he thought of Georgianna pleasuring him, as she was now doing with each slow and delicious swipe of her tongue, the pleasure so intense he could already feel the start of his climax in the tightening, drawing up of his balls.

His gaze dropped to her bared breasts visible through the silky curtain of her hair as they jutted free of her unfastened gown as she bent over him. He wanted to hold them. To caress and squeeze them.

As he came and came!

'Come up here, Georgia,' he groaned urgently even as he lifted her up and over him so that she now had a leg either side of his thighs on the chaise. He pushed her dress up to her hips before lowering her down on top of him, not penetrating her, but arching into her in a slow rhythm as her moist and heated folds rubbed caressingly along the sensitised length of his erection.

'Zachary.'

'Do not worry I shall put you at risk, Georgianna,' he assured gruffly, eyes feeling hot and fevered. 'I merely wish to feel your heat upon me. Oh, that feels so damned good!' The hardness of his length moved easily against the slickness of her juices. 'So, so good!' He reached up to cup and squeeze her breasts, to caress and flick his fingernails against those jutting and sensitive nipples.

Georgianna clutched on to Zachary's chest for support, her head feeling dizzy with her own pleasure as Zachary continued to arch and thrust beneath her, even as he caressed and pinched her engorged and sensitive nipples to the exact same rhythm as the hard length of his erection rubbed against her folds and that sensitive nubbin above.

'Harder, Georgia. Faster. Harder again,' he urged, his eyes glittering, a flush to the hardness of his cheeks. 'Come with me, Georgia. Now!' he urged fiercely, sculptured lips parted as his hips surged up in the most powerful thrust of all.

Georgianna had no time to think about what he meant by that as her own pleasure ripped through and over her as the heated jets of Zachary's release pounded against her own sensitive nubbin, prolonging that pleasure until she screamed his name as he now hoarsely shouted hers.

Chapter Twelve

'Georgia?' she questioned Zachary as she lay on the chaise in his arms in the aftermath of their love-making. She felt physically sated and still inwardly moved at the way in which Zachary had kissed that unsightly scar upon her chest.

'You do not like it?' He played absently with the long strands of her loosened ebony hair as he turned to look at her.

No one had ever shortened her name in quite that way before now. Jeffrey often called her Georgie when they were alone together, in remembrance of their time together in the nursery. Her father, when he was alive, had occasionally addressed her affectionately as Anna, which had been her mother's name. But she could not recall her name ever being shortened to Georgia before now, no.

Before Zachary.

And she did like it. Coming from this man, she

found she liked that familiarity. A lot. That she liked, even loved, Zachary a lot, too.

She had no idea when the liking, the admiration, for the strong and determined man that he was, had happened, let alone whether or not she loved all of him. Or how it could possibly have happened, if that was the case.

Zachary had more or less kidnapped her, then kept her a prisoner in his home.

He had ridiculed and insulted her.

And then he had made love to her.

Which was when the liking had begun, Georgianna now realised.

Because when Zachary made love to her he forgot to insult and ridicule her. To dislike her. Most of all, he was a generous and fulfilling lover. Oh, that first time might have begun as a punishment for her, for daring to elope with another man when she was betrothed to him. But Zachary's generosity of nature, his own physical enjoyment of her, had quickly overcome that emotion.

And today, despite knowing of that disfiguring scar, he truly had made love to her, had kissed and caressed that scar as if it were something to admire rather than be disgusted by.

As Georgianna had made love to him?

She shied away from so much as thinking of that emotion in connection to Zachary Black, the Duke of Hawksmere—the very same man whom she had once shied away from marrying—knowing that to love him would lead to even more heartbreak than had her ill-fated and humiliating elopement with André Rousseau.

'I do not dislike it,' she answered Zachary non-committally, only to look up at him quizzically as he began to chuckle softly. 'What is it?'

'I laugh because, as usual, your thoughts and emotions remain a mystery to me, Georgia.' He gazed down at her indulgently.

She frowned her puzzlement. 'I do not mean them to be.'

'Any more than I believe just now to have been my finest hour.' He had sobered slightly, a teasing smile now curving those sculptured lips.

'I do not understand?' Everything had seemed more than satisfactory to Georgianna. Very much so. 'Did I do something wrong?' she prompted anxiously.

'Lord, no.' He groaned his reassurance. 'If you had done anything more right, then I believe I might now be lying here dead from a heart attack.'

She blushed at his effusive praise for her lovemaking. 'Then I still do not understand.'

Zachary could see that she really had no idea what he was talking about. Had Rousseau been such a uninterested and unsatisfactory lover that even Zachary's hasty lovemaking just now was preferable? Hasty, because his thoughts of Georgianna these past two weeks had caused him to hope, to anticipate, the worshipping of every inch of her delectable and responsive body. To kiss and caress her. To give her pleasure again and again.

Instead Georgianna had taken control of the situation, of him, and made love to him in a way that had surpassed all and any of his fantasies of being with her again.

He grimaced. 'We might have expected our love-making to last for longer than a few minutes,' he explained gruffly. 'I had expected my own control to last for longer than a few minutes,' he added ruefully. 'I wanted it to be enjoyable for you, too.'

'How could you ever imagine it was not enjoyable for me, too, when I cried out my pleasure?' Her cheeks blushed a becoming rose.

'Because I know it could have been better.' He caressed that blush upon her cheeks. 'I could have been better. Instead, I was as out of control as a callow youth being touched by a woman for the first time.' Indeed, he had been lost the moment he had felt the soft fullness of Georgianna's lips upon him, and the soft rasp of her tongue as she licked and tasted him; at that moment he'd had no more control than the night he had lost his virginity fifteen years ago.

'What was your finest hour?' Georgianna now prompted almost warily.

Zachary knew she was questioning him about his previous physical experiences. Unnecessarily, as it happened, because enjoyable as those past encounters might have been, none of them had affected him in the way that making love to and with Georgianna did. And that was without his having as yet fully made love to her, because he had yet to bury himself in the heat and lushness of her.

Even this, their closeness now as they cuddled in

each other's arms in the aftermath of that lovemaking, was an unusual occurrence for Zachary. Usually he could not vacate a woman's bed quickly enough once the deed was done.

This closeness with Georgianna was one he cherished rather than wished to avoid.

At the same time he knew that he must now put an end to that closeness. That he had yet to tell Georgianna of his encounter with Rousseau in Paris.

And he had no idea how she would react, what she would say, once she knew her previous lover was now dead.

Admittedly, Rousseau had treated her abominably, had seduced her, deceived her, betrayed her, before believing he had killed her.

But love, the emotions of a woman's heart, were not things Zachary was familiar with, either. Despite all that Rousseau had done to her, Georgianna might still feel some vestige of that emotion for the other man. Knowing that Zachary had been instrumental in his demise might shatter this unique, and highly enjoyable, time between the two of them.

Did he want to risk that, put an end to this time of harmony between the two of them, for the sake of honesty?

No.

But if he chose not to, then how could he ever reassure Georgianna that she no longer had anything to fear from Rousseau? Or expect Georgianna's forgiveness, when she eventually learnt, as she surely must, that he had kept this information from her and for such selfish reasons?

No, he could not keep Rousseau's death to himself. He knew he must share that news with Georgianna.

Even at the risk of bringing an end to the fragile intimacy that now existed between the two of them.

Reluctantly he pulled his arms from around her, removing his handkerchief from his pocket and gently mopping up the worst of the evidence of their love-making, before standing up to turn away and refasten his clothing. He ran agitated hands through the tousled length of his hair as he contemplated how to begin this next conversation.

'Zachary?' Georgianna eyed him uncertainly as she slowly sat up, continuing to look at him even as she absently refastened the buttons on the front of her gown. Her hair was beyond repair at this moment, the pins scattered about the floor from when Zachary had released it earlier.

The lover of just moments ago was gone. Zachary's expression was guarded when he turned back to face her and flatly announced. 'Georgianna, there is no other way for me to tell you this. My dear, Rousseau is dead.'

She felt the colour leach from her cheeks even as she swayed slightly where she sat, unable to believe, to process the enormity of what Zachary was saying to her.

André was dead?

How was such a thing even possible?

André was still a young man, aged only seven and twenty, and in the best of health when she had last seen him just weeks ago, so his death could not possibly have been through natural causes.

Her gaze sharpened on Zachary, his own eyes, as he met her horrified gaze, a pale and glittering silver in his harshly forbidding face. 'You killed him.' It was not a question, but a statement.

Zachary's expression was grim. 'Unfortunately I did not have that particular honour.'

'But you were responsible for ordering his death?' She could see the answer to that accusation in the tightening of Zachary's jaw and the arrogant challenge now in those eyes, as he looked down at her through narrowed lids.

Zachary had instructed André should be killed.

The question was, why had he done so?

Because the other man had been shown to be Napoleon's spy and in part responsible for the Corsican's escape from Elba?

Or because of a reason more personal to Zachary, in that the other man had taken something of his, had taken Georgianna, when he eloped with her?

She somehow doubted very much it had anything to do with the other man hurting and having attempted to kill Georgianna after they had arrived in France.

The first of those reasons, at least, would be honourable. To have someone killed out of a sense of personal vengeance would not.

She looked up at Zachary searchingly, but could read nothing from the harshness of his expression, could only see the challenge in the set of his shoulders beneath his superfine and his stance: legs slightly parted as he stood on booted feet, his hands clasped together behind the broadness of his back.

Leaving Georgianna in absolutely no doubt that whatever his reason for having André dispatched, Zachary did not feel a moment's remorse over it.

And nor should Georgianna.

But, no matter how cruel and deceitful as André had been, murderously so, and despite the freedom from future fear his death now gave her, Georgianna still could not find cause for celebration. Not for André's demise, nor the fact that Zachary was tacitly admitting to being the one responsible for ordering that death, if not the reason for it.

His mouth twisted derisively now. 'I had expected a happier response from you upon hearing this news?' he drawled mockingly.

Georgianna drew in a ragged breath before speaking. 'Why did you wait until now to tell me?'

'Sorry?' Zachary frowned darkly at the question.

Georgianna lifted her shoulders. 'Why did you wait, until after we had made love, to tell me?'

'It was not a conscious decision.'

'Are you sure of that?' she scorned. 'Could it be that the delay was because you knew I would not wish, or have the inclination, to make love with you once I knew?' she guessed shrewdly.

He gave a shake of his head. 'Georgianna—'

'Why did you do it, Zachary?' Georgianna pushed determinedly, deciding she could not think of Zachary's duplicity now. That she would think of it later. Much later.

'I do not recall admitting that I am the one responsible for Rousseau's death.' He arched arrogant dark brows over those now arctic-grey eyes.

No, he had not. And yet, still, Georgianna knew instinctively that he was. That the Zachary standing before her now, every inch one of the cold and remote Dangerous Dukes, was more than capable of killing if called upon to do so. That he had no doubt killed many men during his years as an agent for the Crown. And lived with the consequences of those deaths without regret or remorse.

But having André Rousseau killed was different to those other deaths. For one thing, they were not yet again at war with Napoleon. And no matter how much Zachary might have assured himself it was necessary to have André killed, it could not change the fact that he had also despised the other man on a very personal level. To the point of seeking out the other man and personally seeing to his demise?

Whatever Zachary's reasons for having dispatched André, Georgianna found she was not as capable as he of placing the events of her life into neatly labelled boxes. She needed time, and solitude, in which to come to terms with what she knew was Zachary's involvement in André's death. 'Were you there when he died?' She looked at Zachary searchingly.

His jaw was tightly clenched. 'Yes. Damn it, Georgianna, the man was a spy against England.'

'And I remind you we are no longer at war with France!'

'We very soon will be again.' A nerve pulsed in that tightly clenched jaw. 'Have you forgotten that just last night you asked that I do all that I can to prevent Jeffrey from becoming embroiled in that war?'

'Do not turn this conversation around on me in that way, Zachary,' she warned through clenched jaw as she stood up abruptly before collecting up her bonnet and gloves. Zachary's words confirmed that at least part of his reasoning for having André killed was because the other man had spied upon England.

Selfishly, perhaps, had she secretly wished that it might have been out of defence of her? She might, with time, have forgiven that. Because it might also have meant that Zachary had perhaps come to care for her as she cared for him.

But the thought that Zachary could have ruthlessly ordered the other man be killed, because of a personal slight against himself, as much as because he was considered to be an enemy of England, was a side of Zachary, that cold and dispassionate side, from which she had run just eleven short months ago.

And from which she must run away again now.

'Where are you going?' Zachary demanded as he watched Georgianna walk to the door of the salon without saying so much as another word to him, her hair a bewitching dark waterfall of curls down the slenderness of her defensively straight spine.

He had half expected this might be Georgianna's

reaction to the news of Rousseau's death. Expected it, but hoped that it would not be so.

Because, he had also hoped, prayed, that she had no softer feelings left inside her for the other man after the abominable way he had treated her. For having attempted to kill her.

Georgianna's reaction now to the news of Rousseau's death, and her obvious disgust with Zachary for what she believed to have been his part in it, now showed him how wrong he had been to harbour even the smallest hope in that regard.

Stupidly, naïvely, because of the warmth of her responses to him earlier, Zachary had harboured another hope, a dream, that all of her softer feelings were now reserved for him.

He had been wrong not to have told her of Rousseau's death immediately—he accepted that now. But he had wanted to hold her in his arms once more at least before he did so, and once he held her in his arms, he'd had no thought for anything else!

An omission for which Georgianna obviously now despised him, as much as she was so obviously distressed at Rousseau's death. She was disgusted, too, with Zachary for what she perceived to be his part in that death.

Because, despite his intentions, he really could not claim to be the one who had delivered the death blow to Rousseau.

Oh, he and Wolfingham had faultlessly carried out their plan for Wolfingham to engage Rousseau and his cohorts when they eventually emerged from his sister's tavern in the early hours of the morning. They had selected Wolfingham because he was unknown to Rousseau, as Zachary was not.

His friend had been the one to weave drunkenly past the inn at the exact moment the group emerged, deliberately knocking into one of them without apology and instantly receiving an aggressively challenging response. At which point Wolfingham had delivered the first punch.

In the mêlée and confusion that followed, Zachary was supposed to emerge from his own shadowed hiding place, to separate Rousseau from his cohorts, before taking him somewhere far quieter than the street, so that the other man might learn exactly the reason he was about to die.

All had gone according to that plan until Rousseau had pulled a gun from within his coat, his obvious intention to dispatch Wolfingham. At which point Wolfingham had no choice but to defend himself. There had been a shot fired as Zachary landed several blows on the other fellows in his efforts to reach his friend's side, but within seconds of the gun being fired, it seemed, the majority of the men had scattered, instantly becoming lost to various parts of the city and leaving behind the two men who lay still upon the ground, their life's blood glistening on the cobbles beneath them.

Rousseau and Wolfingham.

Zachary's own heart had ceased beating in his chest as he rushed to his friend's side and had only started again once he had roused Wolfingham and had satisfied himself that his friend's gunshot wound to the shoulder was nasty, but thankfully did not appear to be life-threatening.

Rousseau had been less fortunate, blood pumping from the artery in his slit throat, his eyes already starting to take on that opaque appearance of one about to die. Nevertheless, he had managed to focus enough to recognise Zachary, a mocking smile curving his lips. 'Hawksmere. I should have known. You are too late, I am afraid—your betrothed is dead,' he managed to taunt gruffly.

Zachary's breath left him in a hiss. 'Is she?' he taunted back angrily. 'I assure you that when I last saw Georgianna, just days ago, she still breathed, and walked, and talked. Mainly she talked of how much she hates you for your failed effort to kill her in a forest outside this very city.'

Surprised blond brows rose above those rapidly glazing blue eyes. 'She still lives?' he croaked, the blood still pumping from his slit throat.

'Oh, yes, despite your intentions for it to be otherwise, Georgianna most assuredly still lives,' Zachary had replied grimly. 'And loves.

'And hates. She also told us a pretty tale about your own involvement with the Corsican's recent departure from Elba.'

The other man gave a gurgling laugh as some of the blood gathered in the back of his throat. 'Georgianna ever saw herself as the heroine.'

'She is a heroine, you bast—'

'Vive Napoleon,' Rousseau murmured with his last

breath, those blue eyes wide as he stared lifelessly up into the darkness of the starlit sky above.

Zachary had left him where he lay in his own blood as he hurried back to Wolfingham's side, putting a supporting arm about his friend as they made good their own escape. The two of them hid at the dockside until it was time for them to board their ship and set sail back to England that same night.

The satisfaction of being able to tell Rousseau, before he died, that Georgianna still lived became a hollow victory as Zachary now saw the way Georgianna looked across the room at him with emotionless eyes.

'I am leaving, of course,' she answered his earlier question flatly. 'I presume informing me of André's death was the reason you wished to speak with me today?' She arched cool brows.

There was such a coolness about her, a distance, that frustrated Zachary intensely. Had he been wrong, misread the situation completely, and Georgianna did indeed still have feelings for the man who had once been her lover?

'You should know I have absolutely no regrets concerning Rousseau's death,' he assured through gritted teeth. Wolfingham had no cause for regrets in the matter, either, had merely been defending himself when Rousseau met his end. If Rousseau had not died, then Wolfingham assuredly would have, and that was totally unacceptable to Zachary. 'A friend of mine was also grievously wounded that night.'

Georgianna frowned slightly. 'Wolfingham?'

'Yes.'

'But he lives still?'

'No thanks to your friend Rousseau.'

'He was never my friend.' Her eyes glittered, with the fierceness of her anger as well as unshed tears. 'I must go.'

'Georgianna!'

She gave a fierce shake of her head. 'We have nothing left to talk about, Hawksmere.'

Addressing him as Hawksmere was indication enough of how Georgianna now felt towards him, the cold dismissal in her tone only adding to that obvious disdain.

And pride, though a cold bedfellow, was preferable to Zachary having his further pleas for her understanding rejected out of hand. 'I will see you again this evening, when I accompany you and Jeffrey to Lady Colchester's musical soirée.'

Georgianna gave a shake of her head. 'I am not sure I feel well enough to attend.'

'You most certainly will attend, Georgianna.' Zachary grated harshly. 'Not only will you attend, but you will also give every appearance of enjoyment in the enterprise. In appearing at my side, along with Jeffrey, as my two wards.'

She raised her chin in challenge. 'I am sure you know me well enough by now, Hawksmere, to know that I shall not be bullied into doing anything I do not wish to do, by you or anyone else.'

His jaw tightened, eyes glittering dangerously. 'Nevertheless, it was planned for this evening to be your first appearance back into society, following your period of mourning. As such, as your guardian, I must insist that you accompany Jeffrey and me.'

She looked across at him searchingly, knowing by the coldness in Zachary's eyes, the bleakness of his expression and the nerve pulsing in the tightness of his jaw, that he meant exactly what he said. Nor could she deny the importance of her appearance at Lady Colchester's tonight, following what many in society believed to have been the ending of her engagement to Hawksmere and her term of mourning her father. 'We shall see,' she finally answered noncommittally.

This young woman would surely be the death of him, Zachary acknowledged impatiently. Either that, or he might go quietly and completely insane.

How could it be that just a few moments ago the two of them had been so enjoyably making love together, as close as any two people could be—certainly as close as Zachary had been to any woman—and now they were as distant as they had been ten months ago? More so, for then Zachary had not really known what it was to be close to Georgianna, had never so much as even spoken to her; now he knew exactly what, and who, he would be losing when she walked out of his life for a second time.

The woman he had come to admire above all others.

Georgianna.

Georgia.

Chapter Thirteen

'I do believe you are alarming our poor hostess with the darkness of your scowls, Zachary,' an amused voice drawled beside him as Zachary stood near one of the windows in Lady Colchester's music room during a break in the entertainments.

His eyes widened as he turned to look at Wolfingham. 'Should you be out and about when you are still recovering from a bullet wound to your shoulder?'

'It would look decidedly odd if I were absent from society for any length of time. Besides which, needs must, I am afraid.' Wolfingham gave a grimace.

'Oh?'

His friend nodded abruptly. 'I do not suppose you have seen anything of my little brother this evening?'

Zachary's brows rose. 'Should I have done?' As far as he was aware, young Lord Anthony Hunter had been fortunate enough not to have put in even a nominal appearance at Lady Colchester's musical soirée.

Not unless he had arrived and left before Zachary and his party arrived.

'Obviously not,' Wolfingham uttered disgustedly. 'Is there a problem?'

'If there is, then it is for me to deal with,' his friend dismissed briskly. 'What were you scowling at so intently just now?' Wolfingham glanced across the room in the direction Zachary had been scowling earlier. 'Who is the honeypot attracting all the bees?'

Zachary did not at all appreciate hearing Georgianna described as a honeypot. Even if that was exactly what she had been from the moment they arrived at Lady Colchester's home several hours ago.

Georgianna was resplendent in a gown of purple silk, a strip of lace styled discreetly across the tops of her breasts, and so concealing that damning scar, with a matching purple feather adorning the darkness of her curls.

They had barely had time to greet their hostess before the first of the handsome young bucks began to flock about them. Most of them acquaintances of her brother, Jeffrey, eager to be re-introduced to his beautiful sister. But there had been some older gentlemen, too. Single gentlemen, of Zachary's own age and older, attracted no doubt by the air of untouchable remoteness with which Georgianna appeared to have steeled herself in order to endure appearing at this evening's entertainment.

A remoteness, which had thawed throughout the evening until, as now, she appeared to be enjoying the attentions of so many handsome gentlemen. The wariness had slowly faded from her gaze, a becoming blush now adorning her cheeks, and those two familiar dimples having appeared in those same cheeks when she smiled, at what were no doubt flattering and flirtatious comments being made to and about her.

And for the whole of this time Zachary had wished for nothing more than to dismiss the attentions of every single one of those handsome and fawning gentlemen, before whisking Georgianna away somewhere they could be private together.

So, yes, Wolfingham's description of his having been scowling minutes ago—enough so as to have warned off the approach of all and any who were not closely acquainted with him, who were very few—was no doubt an accurate one.

'My ward, Lady Georgianna Lancaster,' he now supplied.

Wolfingham continued to look at Georgianna consideringly. 'This is the same young woman to whom you were so briefly betrothed last year?'

'Yes.'

The other man's brows rose. 'She appears to be much changed from a year ago.'

Zachary's mouth tightened at the reasons for those changes, in both Georgianna's appearance and demeanour. 'She is, yes.'

Wolfingham turned to look at him through narrowed lids. 'I was not just referring to the more obvious changes in her appearance.'

A nerve pulsed in Zachary's jaw, knowing that his friend was able to detect the air of remoteness, and the sophistication, which had been so lacking in Georgianna just a year ago. 'No.'

'Zachary.'

'I would prefer not to discuss my ward any further,' he warned harshly. 'Even with you.'

Wolfingham continued to study him for several long seconds before nodding slowly. 'If you will just answer one more question?'

Zachary scowled his irritation. 'Which is?'

'Does she know that Rousseau is dead?'

'Yes, she knows.' Zachary did not attempt to pretend to misunderstand Wolfingham, knew that his friend had guessed, correctly, that Georgianna Lancaster was the woman whom Rousseau had treated so despicably. The reason the other man had to die.

'You like her?' Wolfingham guessed astutely.

Zachary's jaw clenched at the understatement. 'I do.'

'Enough to consider renewing your betrothal?'

His jaw clenched. 'There is absolutely no chance of that ever happening.'

'None?'

The nerve in his jaw pulsed even more rapidly. 'None whatsoever.'

'Time is passing, Zachary, and the condition in your father's will that states you must marry and produce an heir before your thirty-fifth birthday remains just as pressing,' Wolfingham reminded softly.

'And Georgianna is the last woman who would ever accept a—another—marriage proposal from me.' Zachary grimaced. 'Indeed, I believe Georgianna despises me more now than she did a year ago.'

Wolfingham sighed heavily. 'Life can be complicated at times, can it not?'

'Very,' Zachary grated.

His friend nodded. 'If you will excuse me, I believe I must continue to search for my own complication.'

Zachary frowned. 'Is Anthony in trouble?'

'Only with me,' Wolfingham assured darkly.

'If you should need any assistance in the matter...'

Wolfingham nodded distractedly. 'For the moment just be grateful you do not have a sibling for whom you are guardian.'

Zachary had very much regretted not having siblings when he was very young, but since meeting his four close friends at school he had not felt that same need, those four gentlemen more than filling that gap in his life. As they had all been there for him when he'd lost his parents when he was a child.

As they all remained there for each other as adults. 'Anthony is not in any danger?' He studied Wolfingham closely.

His friend's mouth thinned. 'Again, only from me. No doubt you have a similar headache, since becoming guardian to the two Lancaster siblings?'

Zachary glanced across at Georgianna once again, eyes glittering as he saw her batting her fan playfully in order to ward off the attentions of one of her more ardent suitors. 'If you will excuse me.' He didn't wait for his friend to reply before marching purposefully across the length of Lady Colchester's music room.

'I believe you are crowding the lady, Adams!' He glared down the length of his nose at the younger man.

Georgianna raised her open fan to hide her surprise as Hawksmere took up a protective stance at her side, his expression grimly forbidding as he glared at the gentlemen surrounding her.

Not that she did not appreciate Zachary having joined her; the gentlemen were becoming more and more persistent in their attentions, several of them currently vying for the honour of dancing the first set with her at the Countess of Evesham's ball tomorrow evening. A ball Georgianna was not sure she wished to attend any more than she had wished to attend this soirée.

This evening had been every bit the ordeal Georgianna had thought it might be.

Being with Hawksmere again had proved to be every bit of the ordeal she had imagined it might be!

It seemed incredible to her that she and Hawksmere had allowed themselves more than once to become embroiled in a situation of deep intimacy. An intensity of intimacy that made her blush with embarrassment every time she so much as thought about it.

And, to her shame, she had been unable to stop herself from thinking about it ever since she and Hawksmere had parted earlier today. Of how he had felt beneath the touch of her hands and lips. How he had tasted.

It had not helped that Zachary had looked, and continued to look, every inch the arrogantly handsome Duke of Hawksmere when he arrived at Malvern House earlier this evening. His muscled physique was shown to advantage in his black evening clothes and snowy white linen, the darkness of his hair arranged in tousled disarray as it curled over his ears and nape and about the sculptured perfection of his face.

Georgianna's heart had skipped several beats when she'd first gazed at him earlier this evening, a reaction she'd been quick to hide as she'd turned to thank her brother as he held out his arm to her in readiness for their departure.

She had deliberately seated herself beside Jeffrey in Hawksmere's carriage, very aware of, and avoiding meeting, the steadiness of Hawksmere's gaze as he sat directly across from her. She had kept her face averted as she looked out the window beside her, pretending an interest in the busy London evening streets.

Only to then find herself accompanied protectively by Jeffrey on one side and Hawksmere on the other, as they had entered Lady Colchester's London home together.

A closeness that had allowed her to feel the warmth emanating from Hawksmere's body through the silk of her gown, to smell his familiar smell of sandalwood and citrus, along with expensive cigars and just a hint of brandy upon his breath.

The latter in evidence, perhaps, that Hawksmere had felt in need of some restorative himself, in order to be able to get through the evening ahead?

Somehow Georgianna doubted that Hawksmere had ever needed a restorative, of any kind, to get through anything.

Nevertheless, Georgianna had felt grateful that the interest and conversation of Jeffrey's friends had separated her from Hawksmere, both before and during this break in the entertainments. His close proximity as they had sat together listening to several of the young ladies perform on their various musical instruments, had disturbed Georgianna on a level she had found distinctly uncomfortable. She still had no idea how she felt about Hawksmere's involvement with André's premature death.

That she no longer had anything to fear, in regard to André ever finding her again, was a relief beyond measure. Nor, having had time to adjust to André's demise, did she find she felt the least regret. How could she regret it, when she had lived in fear of discovery by him these past months? No, it was Hawksmere's involvement in the other man's death which still unsettled her.

Frightened her?

No, she was not frightened by the thought of such violence. She was sure that most men, and women, were capable of committing murder if pushed to the extreme. That she had been more than capable, given the weapon to do so, of killing André herself that night in the woods outside Paris, when he had tried to end her life.

But if she had succeeded in killing André, then it would have been an act of desperation on her part, of self-survival, rather than the cold-blooded murder she suspected his death to have been.

'If you gentlemen will excuse us?' Zachary's narrowed gaze precluded there being any objections to his announcement as he took a firm hold of Georgianna's arm to walk purposefully across to the other side of the room, well out of earshot of Lady Colchester's other guests. A frown darkened his brow as he now looked down at Georgianna through narrowed lids.

'You are hurting my arm, Hawksmere.' She gazed up at him steadily, pointedly, while all the time keeping a smile of politeness upon her lips for the benefit of their audience. The curious glances in their direction by the ladies present were surreptitious, but there nonetheless. No doubt due to the fact that the two of them had once been betrothed to be married. To each other.

Zachary lessened his grip, but refused to release her completely, at the same time as his own expression remained one of bland politeness. No doubt also for the benefit of their audience. 'I realise I am not your favourite person, Georgianna, but I do not think that ignoring me is in any way going to help quell the gossip, as this evening was predisposed to do, regarding our past broken betrothal,' he muttered impatiently.

Zachary believed he was not her favourite person?

Georgianna's feelings in regard to Hawksmere were now in such confusion that she no longer had any idea what she felt towards him. Despite the fact that he only had to touch her, it seemed, for her to melt into his arms.

Surely her reaction could be termed as being merely a physical response to a handsome and desirable gentleman?

Merely?

Her responses to Zachary were above and beyond anything Georgianna had ever experienced in her life before him. Not even that imagined love for André had filled her with such longings, such desires, as she felt when Zachary took her in his arms and kissed and caressed her.

Longings, and a desire, she had no right to feel for a man who would never be—could never be anything more to her than her reluctant guardian. And even that tenuous connection would very soon cease to exist.

Her chin rose defensively now. 'Is it not enough that I am here, as you instructed me to be? I do not recall your having said I had to enjoy or like it?' she added pointedly.

Zachary drew in an impatient breath. 'You appeared to be enjoying the attentions of those other gentlemen just a few minutes ago.'

Georgianna arched a brow. 'Was that not what I was supposed to do?'

As far as Zachary was concerned? No, it was not. In fact, he found he did not enjoy having any other gentleman within ten feet of Georgianna.

His jaw tightened. 'I do not think it a particularly good idea for you to encourage a repeat of society's past belief in your reputation as being something of a flirt.'

Her eyes widened with indignation. 'You— I— You are insulting, sir!'

Deliberately so, Zachary acknowledged heavily. And knowing he was not endearing himself to Georgianna in the slightest by acting the part of the jealous lover.

Even if he knew that's exactly how he felt.

He had hated every moment of watching Georgianna being flattered and admired by those other gentlemen this evening. Had wanted nothing more than to sweep her up in his arms and carry her off to a place no other man could look at her, let alone flatter and charm her into possibly falling in love with him.

Quite what Zachary was going to do about the heat of his own emotions in regard to Georgianna he had no idea, when she now gave every impression of disliking him intensely.

Was he, as her guardian, to be forced to stand silently by whilst some other man charmed and flattered her into falling in love with him?

Would he then have to welcome that suitor into his own home, when that gentleman came to ask his permission for seeking Georgianna's hand in marriage?

Impossible.

Just the thought of it was enough to cause Zachary's hand to clench into a fist at his side. He would not, could not, allow it. 'Are you ready to leave this insipid entertainment?' he prompted harshly.

Violet-coloured eyes widened in the pallor of

Georgianna's face. 'If you have somewhere else you wish to go, then I am sure Jeffrey is more than capable of acting as my chaperon for the rest of the evening.'

'The only somewhere else I wish us both to go is far away from here!' Zachary bit out harshly, only to draw in a long and calming breath as Georgianna's face became even paler at his vehemence. 'I believe we need to talk further, Georgianna,' he added softly.

Her brows rose. 'About what, exactly?'

'In private.' A nerve pulse in his tightly clenched jaw. If he did not find himself alone with Georgianna in the next few minutes then he was afraid he was going to do something that would cause them both embarrassment. Not that he cared on his own behalf, but Georgianna was likely to be less forgiving if he caused a scene on her very first evening back into society.

And a Georgianna who felt angry and resentful towards him was not what he wished for at all.

Georgianna eyed Zachary warily, not sure that she wished to be anywhere private with him, when he was in his current mood of unpredictability. Not that he had ever been in the least predictable to her, but there was such an air of tension about him this evening she felt even more wary of him than she had in the past.

'To what purpose?' she persisted guardedly.

A nerve pulsed in his throat. 'Does it matter?'

'Yes, of course it matters,' Georgianna answered irritably. 'As you have already pointed out, this is my first venture back into society, and my leaving with you now, halfway through the entertainments, would seem… It would look improper,' she concluded lamely.

It was possible to hear Hawksmere's teeth grinding together. 'Then let it.'

Georgianna's eyes widened in alarm. 'Can it be that you are foxed, Hawksmere? I seem to recall I thought I could smell brandy upon your breath when you arrived at Malvern House earlier this evening.'

'I am most assuredly not foxed, nor do I have any intentions of being so,' he bit out harshly. 'I am merely expressing a wish for the two of us to leave this hellish torture and go somewhere where we might talk privately together.'

Her brows rose. 'I do not recall your having been so eager, or particularly interested, in anything I had to say to you in the past.' She felt no qualms in reminding him that he had not so much as had a conversation with her before offering her marriage mere months ago. Or of his distrust of her, and of the information she'd wished to impart to him, when she'd first returned to England just weeks ago.

Was it really only three weeks since she had secretly returned to England? So much had happened in that time it seemed so much longer.

Zachary knew that he well deserved Georgianna's criticism. But he wished to remedy those wrongs now. He wanted to make amends for his past arrogance and thoughtlessness. If Georgianna would only allow it.

'I freely acknowledge that I have behaved appallingly towards you in the past, Georgianna.'

'How gracious of you to admit it!'

Zachary closed his eyes briefly as he heard the sarcasm underlying Georgianna's tone. As he inwardly fought to hold on to what little temper he had left. 'I am asking, politely, that you now leave this place with me, Georgianna, in order that we might talk together in calmness and—'

'This hellish place?' she interrupted tauntingly.

It had been hellish for him to have to sit at Georgianna's side and listen to the often painful musical efforts of half a dozen twittering young women, all of them hoping to impress the gentlemen present with their questionable talents. A so-called entertainment which Zachary would never have bothered himself to suffer through in the past and had only done so this evening as an open support of Georgianna's return to society.

But enough was enough, as far as Zachary was concerned; he simply could not sit through another minute of either of those painful entertainments, or Georgianna's coolly distant presence, as she sat silent and unmoving beside him. Nor could he witness further demonstration of the attentions of other men.

'Do not pretend you have the least interest in listening to any more of this unholy caterwauling,' he muttered disgustedly.

Georgianna quickly caught her top lip between her teeth in an effort to hold back her humour at Hawksmere's characteristic, and totally familiar, rudeness. A rudeness she far more readily understood than the intensity of emotions which seemed to be bubbling beneath the surface of Hawksmere's present mood of restless impatience.

'That is very ungentlemanly of you, Hawksmere,' she murmured reprovingly.

'The truth often is,' he came back unrepentantly.

The truth.

What was the truth of her feelings for Hawksmere? Did she loathe him or love him? She had once loathed him with a passion, enough so as to have eloped with another man, rather than become his wife. Her responses to Zachary since her return to England, the way she trembled even now just at his close proximity, said she no longer felt the least loathing for him, that her emotions now moved in another direction entirely.

Towards love?

For Hawksmere?

If that was truly what she felt for him then she must still be as stupidly naïve as she had been in the past. Certainly more so even than she had been eleven months ago, when she had believed herself to be in love with and loved by André!

Until now she had believed that to have been her defining moment of *naïveté*, but it was as nothing compared to the self-inflicted torture if she had indeed allowed herself to fall in love with Zachary Black. There could be nothing but pain and disillusionment from loving a man such as he. A man so cynical, so indifferent to the emotion of love, he had thought nothing of tying himself for life to, of marrying, a young woman he had not so much as had an interest in speaking privately to or with before offering for her.

And yet he was expressing a wish to talk privately with that same young woman now.

Perhaps so, but it was no doubt only because she had brought an abrupt end to their conversation earlier regarding André's death. A subject about which Georgianna had no desire to hear, or learn, any more than she already did. André was dead, by whatever means, and she did not need to know, could not bear to know, any more on the subject.

She straightened her spine determinedly. 'I am afraid it is not possible for me to leave just yet, your Grace.' She ignored the way Hawksmere's mouth tightened at her deliberate formality. 'My friend Charlotte Reynolds is about to play the pianoforte in the second half of the entertainments and I have already promised her I will stay long enough to listen.'

Zachary snorted his frustration with this development. 'And our own conversation?'

She shrugged uninterestedly. 'Will just have to wait.'

Zachary did not want to wait. Did not want to share Georgianna for another minute longer. With her friends. Her brother. Or the dozen or so eager young bucks watching them so curiously from across the room. No doubt all waiting for the moment they could pounce upon Georgianna again. If there was any pouncing to be done, then Zachary wished it to be only by him!

What he really wanted to do was to once again

make Georgianna a prisoner in his bedchamber. To keep her there, making love to and with her, until she did not have the strength to even think of leaving him again.

It was a side of himself Zachary did not recognise. A side of himself which he was uncertain he wished to recognise.

His mouth thinned. 'You are refusing to leave with me?'

'I believe I must, yes.' Georgianna gave him an impatient glance as his scowl of displeasure deepened. 'You are acting very strangely this evening, Hawksmere.'

No doubt. He felt very strange, too. Felt most uncomfortable with the uncharacteristic emotions churning inside him. There was most certainly impatience at their surroundings. That restlessness to be alone with Georgianna. The desire to make love to her again. And that interminable, unacceptable jealousy of the other men, just waiting for the opportunity to fawn over and flatter her.

What did it all mean? This turmoil of emotions, this possessiveness he now felt towards Georgianna?

Until he knew the answer to those questions, perhaps he should not talk privately with Georgianna, after all, but instead go to his club? Perhaps with the intention of imbibing too much brandy? If only as a means of dulling this turmoil of unfathomable emotions that held him so tightly in its grip.

He removed his hand from the top of Georgianna's

arm as he stepped back to bow formally. 'I will wish you a goodnight, then, Georgianna.'

Georgianna blinked her surprise at the abruptness of Zachary's sudden capitulation to her refusal to leave with him, when just seconds ago he had seemed equally as determined that she would do so.

Would she ever understand this man?

Probably not, she conceded wearily. 'Goodnight, your Grace.'

She bowed her head as she curtsied just as formally.

'Georgianna.'

She glanced up at Hawksmere from beneath lowered lashes as she slowly straightened. 'Yes?'

A nerve pulsed in his tightly clenched jaw, his face pale, a fevered glitter in the paleness of his silver eyes as the words seems forced out of him rather than given willingly. 'Never mind,' he muttered, his gaze no longer meeting hers. 'I wish you joy for the rest of your evening.' He gave another curt bow. 'If you will excuse me? I will inform Jeffrey of my early departure.'

She nodded. 'Your Grace.'

Zachary had never felt such heaviness in his chest before as he now felt walking away from Georgianna in search of Jeffrey Lancaster. He felt strangely as if he were leaving a part of himself behind. A very vital part. Almost as if he might never see Georgianna again after this evening. Which was ridiculous, when he was to be her guardian for another three months at least.

'I believe you and I need to talk privately, Hawks-mere.'

Zachary turned at the harsh sound of his younger ward's voice, eyes narrowing as he took in the angry expression on Jeffrey Lancaster's youthfully handsome face.

'Is there a problem, Jeffrey?' he prompted warily, wondering if Jeffrey had witnessed the tension just now between his sister and Zachary.

The younger man's face flushed with displeasure. 'I did not mean— It was not done intentionally— I had thought to join you and Wolfingham earlier and…I inadvertently overheard part of your conversation,' he bit out accusingly.

And, as Zachary so clearly recalled, any part of his private conversation with Wolfingham would be considered damning to a third party. Most particularly Wolfingham having spoken of the conditions of Zachary's father's will, as being the reason for his betrothal and intended marriage to Jeffrey's sister eleven months ago.

Chapter Fourteen

Zachary slouched down in the chair beside the fireplace at his club as he stared down morosely into the bottom of his empty glass. A glass which seemed to have been emptied of brandy far too often these past few hours.

The club was much quieter than it had been when he arrived here after leaving Lady Colchester's musical soirée, the group of gentlemen who had been playing cards upon his arrival, having long departed. In fact, the club seemed to have emptied almost completely now that Zachary took the trouble to take stock of his surroundings. Something he had certainly not noticed before now, lost in the darkness of his own thoughts as he had been, and still was.

He continued to frown as he filled his glass again from the decanter on the table beside him. The alcohol dulled his senses, if it had not settled the confusion of his thoughts.

Of one thing he was absolutely certain, however: Georgianna now hated him.

And what reason had Zachary provided for her not to feel that way?

He had not so much as given a thought to Georgianna's feelings when he made his offer of marriage to her father eleven months ago. Had thought only of his own needs then and assumed that Georgianna would be flattered by the offer, and more than content just to become a duchess, as most young women of his acquaintance would have been.

Zachary had not realised, had not known then, that Georgianna was not like other young women and had a definite mind of her own in regard to what she wanted for her future. And duke or not, a loveless marriage to Zachary Black had certainly not been what she had wanted.

Zachary was not the man she had wanted, either.

And he was still not the man she wanted in her life.

To a degree that Georgianna did not just scorn him, but now heartily disliked him.

Why that should disturb him, hurt him, quite so much as it did was still something of a mystery to him.

Zachary had always lived his life exactly as he pleased, answerable to no one since his parents died. He did not understand why Georgianna's good opinion should now be of more importance to him than anything or anyone else.

He gave a shake of his head in an effort to clear his mind. But, damn it, what did it mean, when thoughts of a certain woman haunted his every waking moment? When just to look at her caused a tightness in his chest? When her unique perfume alone succeeded in arousing him?

When wanting Georgianna, desiring her, now consumed him utterly?

It was thoughts of their explosive and satisfying lovemaking which had made Zachary's torment this evening all the deeper. Far better that he had never known the softness of Georgianna's lips against his flesh, the caress of her hands upon his body. How he wished he'd never touched the silkiness of her own skin and enjoyed her own unique taste. Better that than to suffer the torment of remembering the way in which Georgianna had withdrawn from him after he had informed her of Rousseau's death.

The shock upon her face yesterday, when he had informed her of that death, her obvious disgust at his own involvement in Rousseau's demise, her coldness towards him since, was proof enough, surely, that she still had feelings for the other man?

And that she would never feel any of those softer feelings in regard to Zachary.

Even more so, now that Malvern had overheard part of Zachary's conversation with Wolfingham earlier this evening. The damning part: when Zachary had discussed the conditions of his father's will and the reason he had offered for Georgianna at all the previous year.

A disclosure that had been the truth then, even if it was not now, and which Zachary had not felt it was within his power to ask Jeffrey to keep from telling his sister.

Even though that truth would no doubt damn him for ever in Georgianna's eyes.

Bastard.

Cold, unfeeling, arrogant, impossible, selfish, selfish bastard!

Georgianna's ire towards Zachary was so intense this evening she did not feel in the least guilty about her repeated use of that unpleasant word inside her head, even as she had danced and flirted with all of the gentlemen at the Countess of Evesham's ball.

As she now muttered several other, stronger, French epithets she had in her vocabulary, as she edged her way round the ballroom of the Countess of Evesham's London home towards the open French doors and the solitude of the terrace beyond.

How could Hawksmere have done such a thing?

To any woman?

To her?

Her conversation with Jeffrey the evening before had revealed that she had been wholly correct in her previous assumptions concerning Hawksmere having calculated intentions when he'd offered marriage to her eleven months ago.

Indeed, it was worse than she had thought, because the offer had been made only so that Hawksmere might attain a wife and impregnate her, and so ensure that his heir was born before his thirty-fifth birthday. And all so that he might inherit all of his father's estate rather than a portion of it.

Poor Jeffrey was most disillusioned with the man he had previously so looked up to and admired.

To Georgianna it explained so much of Zachary's behaviour eleven months ago, of course. The reason he had offered marriage at all to a woman he did not even know and so obviously did not care to know. Followed by his anger that she had then chosen to elope with another man rather than marry him. And his distrust and punishment of her for that misdeed upon her return to England.

No doubt it also explained the penchant Hawksmere had for making love to her. As an example to her, no doubt, as a lesson to her never to cross a duke.

And Hawksmere had dared to be angry with her when they met again? To punish her?

How she despised him now.

Hated him.

Wished him consigned to the devil.

'Where are you going?'

Georgianna came to an abrupt halt, unable to keep the surprised expression from her face as she now turned to see the man who so occupied her thoughts.

Primarily because Hawksmere was not supposed to be at the Countess of Evesham's ball at all this evening. He had sent a note to Malvern House late this afternoon to inform Georgianna and Jeffrey that he would not be attending. He had offered no explanation, but had ended the brief note by wishing them both a pleasant evening.

That he was now standing before her, after all, caused Georgianna's heart to flutter erratically in her chest as she gazed up at him from beneath the fan of her lowered lashes.

He looked magnificent, of course, in his black evening clothes and snowy white linen, a diamond pin glittering amongst the intricate folds of his cravat, his fashionably tousled hair appearing as dark as a raven's wing in the bright candlelit ballroom.

And yet beneath that magnificence Georgianna noted the lines of strain around Zachary's eyes and etched beside the firm line of his mouth, the skin stretched tautly across the pallor of his chiselled cheeks. His mouth was set grimly, eyes glittering that intense silver as he continued to look down at her intently.

She moistened her lips before answering. 'I was going outside on to the terrace to take the air.'

He nodded abruptly. 'Then I will join you.' He took a firm hold of her elbow before cutting a determined swathe through the other guests towards the doors leading outside.

A determination none present dare question and leaving Georgianna no choice but to accompany him.

She was not sure she wished to be alone on the terrace with Zachary, or anywhere else.

Her conversation with Jeffrey the evening before, the confirmation of Hawksmere's perfidy, had cut into her almost with a pain of the same terrible intensity as when André had shot her. Starkly revealing, to Georgianna at least, that she had been using the anger she felt towards Zachary as a defence to hide what she really felt for him.

Love.

How it had happened, why it had happened, she had absolutely no idea, but during the events of the past year she had promised herself, if she survived, that she would never deceive or lie to herself again. And somehow, in these past three weeks, she had managed to fall in love.

She was in love, deeply and irrevocably, with Zachary Black, the emotionally aloof and coldly arrogant Duke of Hawksmere.

The same man who, it now transpired, had only offered for her the previous year because of his father's will. A man who had made it more than obvious, now as then, that he did not believe in love, let alone have any intention of so much as pretending to ever have felt that emotion in regard to Georgianna.

She glanced across at him now as he stood beside her in the moonlight, her expression guarded. 'Your note said that you would not be attending the ball this evening.'

Zachary gave a humourless smile. 'Obviously it is not only a lady's prerogative to change her mind.' In truth, he had regretted sending the note to Malvern and his sister almost the moment it had left his house earlier today, meaning, as it surely did, that he would now have no opportunity in which to see Georgianna today.

At the time of writing the note, Zachary had been feeling decidedly under the weather, his head fit to burst from the copious amount of brandy he had consumed the night before. Even the thought of attending the tedium of a ball increased the pounding inside his head.

Until Hinds, with his usual foresight, had provided Zachary with one of his cure-alls and, in doing so, managed to alleviate that pounding headache to a more manageable level. At which time Zachary had deeply regretted having ever informed Jeffrey and Georgianna that he would not be attending the ball with them this evening, after all.

'I do not think it altogether proper for the two of us to be out here alone together.'

Zachary scowled. 'I am your guardian.'

'And that distinction surely covers a multitude of sins!' she came back sharply.

One of those sins surely being Zachary having made love to her. 'Georgianna…'

'Could we please not argue again tonight, Zachary?' she requested wearily. 'I fear I am not feeling strong enough to deal with our usual thrust and parry this evening.'

Zachary looked at her searchingly, easily noting the pallor of her cheeks. 'Are you feeling unwell?' He swallowed. 'Perhaps because you are mourning Rousseau's death?'

'No!' Georgianna assured vehemently.

The duke looked puzzled. 'And yet it so obviously distressed you when I informed you of his demise yesterday afternoon.'

She moistened dry lips. 'I am, of course, sorry to

hear of the death of any man or woman, but I cannot in all conscience say I am sorry that André is no longer here to torment or frighten me.'

'But you blame me still for instigating that death.'

She had never blamed him for André's death, only questioned the reasoning behind it. But to reveal that to Zachary now must surely also reveal the depth of her own feelings for him.

A depth of feeling he so obviously did not return, nor would he ever do so.

In the circumstances, it was humiliating enough, surely, that she had now realised she had fallen in love with the man she'd once so passionately despised. Surely she did not need for Zachary to be made aware of her humiliation, too?

'Georgianna?' he prompted softly now.

She gave a dismissive shake of her head as she avoided looking into that searching silver gaze. 'I blame no one for André's death but André himself.'

He let out a shaky breath. 'I wish I could believe that was true.'

'You may be assured that it is. I was shocked to learn of his death, nothing more. But I believe I must go back inside now,' she added quickly as she realised he was about to question her further on the subject. 'It is somewhat colder out here than I had realised.'

'Here, take my jacket.' Zachary began to shrug his shoulders out of the close-fitting garment.

'No.' Georgianna had taken a horrified step backwards at the suggestion. She was already completely physically aware of Zachary, of his closeness, his warmth, his tempting masculinity, without being surrounded by the warmth and smell of him, too, as she would be if he were to now place his jacket about her shoulders. 'I really must go back inside.' She took another step back.

Zachary sighed heavily, as he obviously saw her efforts to put yet more distance between them. 'If it is not Rousseau causing you to now flinch away from me, then I can only presume— Jeffrey lost no time last night in informing you of the conditions of my father's will, I take it?' A nerve pulsed in his tightly clenched jaw.

Her chin rose. 'No.'

He nodded. 'There is no excuse for the selfishness of my actions last year. I deeply regret— I am sorry for— Damn it, would you perhaps consider forgiving me if I were to get down on my knees and beg?' he grated harshly, eyes glittering fiercely in the moonlight.

Exactly what was Zachary asking forgiveness for?

For that cold and cynical offer of marriage he had made for her last year?

For his distrust and mistreatment of her when she'd returned to England three weeks ago?

For having made love to her so exquisitely that just to be near him again now made her tremble with that knowledge?

For being complicit in, if not personally responsible, for André's death?

For having made her fall in love with him?

Georgianna had already forgiven Zachary for

those other things, but the love she now felt for him, a love she knew he would never return, was like a painful barb in her chest. And would, she believed, remain so for the rest of her life.

It was not Zachary's fault she had fallen in love with him, of course, but…

To have Zachary get down on his knees in front of her for any reason? To hear him beg for her forgiveness?

No.

Never!

It was unthinkable in such an aristocratic and proud man.

In the man she now realised she loved with all her heart.

'No,' she answered decisively. 'Can you not see how impossible it all is, Zachary?' she added forcefully as he scowled darkly. 'That apologies between us now are— That on their own they are not enough?'

Zachary had nothing else to offer Georgianna but his sincere contrition for any and all of his past misdeeds to her. A contrition Georgianna now made it obvious she neither wanted nor wished to hear. It was as he had suspected: Georgianna could never forgive him. For any of his actions, in the past, or now.

He had thought long and hard today on his confusion of thoughts at his club the previous night. On what that confusion of feelings, he now felt towards Georgianna, might mean.

The answer had been so shocking that he had sat alone in his study for hours after the truth had hit him squarely between the eyes, totally stunned, at the realisation that he had fallen in love with Georgianna.

He had come here this evening in the hope that if Georgianna would at least allow him to apologise, if he could perhaps persuade her into not hating him, that he could then be content with his lot in life. That he could then accept the little she was prepared to give him, as his ward, and perhaps even as his friend.

Instead he now found he could not. That he wanted so much more from Georgianna than her forgiveness, or her lukewarm friendship. That he wanted all or nothing.

And this conversation with Georgianna told him it was to be nothing.

He straightened abruptly. 'It only remains for me to bid you goodnight, then, Georgianna.'

She raised startled lids. 'You are leaving?'

Zachary nodded stiffly. 'My only reason for coming here this evening was to talk to you. To ask your forgiveness. To see if— In the hope that—' His jaw tightened as he broke off abruptly.

He had been completely serious in his offer to Georgianna just now, had been fully prepared to get down on his knees and beg her forgiveness for his past actions, if it would in any way help to change how Georgianna now felt towards him. If he could ask for her friendship, at least. Her definitive reply had assured him there was no hope even of that.

Better by far, then, that he should now withdraw and leave Georgianna to enjoy the rest of the evening, to allow her to blossom and glow under the attentions of the other gentlemen present. One of whom she would no doubt one day fall in love with and marry.

'I do apologise, Georgianna.' He held himself stiffly, unable to so much as think of Georgianna being married to another man. 'For all and every wrong I have ever done you. And now, pray be assured, I will not bother you again on this, or any other subject you find so unpleasant.' He bowed formally before turning on his heel and abruptly leaving the terrace.

Zachary had spoken with such finality that Georgianna could not mistake his words for anything other than what they were. An end to any hope of there ever being so much as a friendship between the two of them.

'Georgie?'

She was totally unaware of the tears falling down her cheeks as she turned to see that her brother, Jeffrey, had now stepped outside on to the terrace. 'Did you hear any of that?' she asked dully.

'Most of it, I believe,' Jeffrey admitted as he crossed the terrace to her side before taking both of her hands in his. He looked down at her searchingly. 'I saw your expression as the two of you left the ballroom together and I was concerned enough to stand guard at the doors, so that I might be close enough to be of assistance if you should have need of me. Your conversation was not at all what I had imagined. Georgie, am I right in thinking you have fallen in love with Hawksmere?'

'Yes.' Georgianna made no attempt to deny it.

Her brother nodded. 'And he obviously has feelings for you.'

'Desire is not enough on its own, Jeffrey,' she assured heavily.

'Are you so certain that is all that Hawksmere feels for you?'

She smiled sadly. 'I am sure you heard Zachary say goodbye to me just now? Not necessarily in words, but in the cold formality of his manner?'

'I heard him saying a reluctant goodbye to you, yes. Georgie—' Jeffrey frowned '—you are much changed since your return from France. You have suffered through so much, more than I know, I am sure. And yet you have survived. More than survived. You have grown into a beautiful and independent woman. More forthright in your manner. Less patient of society's strictures and more determined where your own wishes are concerned.'

'Yes.' Again Georgianna did not attempt to deny it; she had indeed become all of those things these past months.

Her brother nodded. 'I have no idea how you and Hawksmere can have become so close in such a short time, but I am young still, Georgie, though I am far from stupid,' he reproved gently as she would have spoken. 'And there is most certainly something between the two of you. An emotion so strong, so intense, that it is possible to feel the tension in the air whenever the two of you are in a room together.'

Her cheeks warmed. 'As I said, desire alone is not enough.'

'I do not believe Hawksmere came here this evening with any intention of making love to you, Georgie,' her brother reasoned softly. 'I heard enough of your conversation to know that he wished only to talk to you. To offer to get down on his knees and beg for your forgiveness, for any and all of his past misdeeds to you, if necessary. Can you not give him some credit for that, at least, Georgie? Some understanding of what it must have cost him, such a proud man, to have offered to do such a thing? And to question why he would have made such a self-demeaning offer of apology to you at all?'

She sighed deeply. 'Who is to know why Hawksmere does anything?'

'You know, Georgia,' Jeffrey chided. 'You know Hawksmere better than anyone, I believe. Is it not time you searched your own heart? That you forgo a little of your own pride? Talk with him again, before the distance between you becomes too wide to ever be crossed,' he urged softly.

Georgianna did not need to search her own heart to know that she was in love with Zachary.

Could she dare to hope, to believe, that his actions tonight implied he might love her in return?

'What do you have to lose, Georgie?' Jeffrey cajoled.

Nothing. She had absolutely nothing left to lose when it came to loving Zachary.

Chapter Fifteen

'Good evening, Hinds.' Georgianna handed her bonnet and cloak to the surprised butler as she stepped past him into the cavernous hallway of Hawksmere House. 'Is his Grace at home?'

The butler looked more than a little flustered by having her arrive at his employer's home at eleven o'clock in the evening. 'He returned some minutes ago and has retired to his study.'

'Which is where?' She gazed pointedly at the half dozen doors leading off the entrance hall.

'The second door on the right. But…'

'Thank you.' Georgianna gave the butler a brightly dismissive smile, determined to go through with her decision to speak with Zachary again. 'Perhaps you might bring through a decanter of brandy?' Bravado had brought her thus far—she did not intend to let it desert her now.

'His Grace has just this minute instructed I do so,

my lady.' Hind's brows were still raised in astonishment at her commanding behaviour.

Understandably so, when she considered the butler was fully aware that she had once been held here as Hawksmere's prisoner.

Although she did feel slightly heartened by the fact that Zachary had obviously felt in need of a restorative brandy—or two—upon his return home. 'I will not delay you from your duties any longer then, Hinds.'

'What on earth is going on, Hinds?' Hawksmere came to an abrupt halt in the now-open doorway of his study, his expression one of stunned disbelief as he gazed across at her.

'Georgianna?'

'Hawksmere.' She managed to greet him with the same brightness as she had addressed the butler seconds ago, determined not to lose her nerve now that she found herself face to face with Zachary.

As Jeffrey had gently chided earlier, the situation between herself and Zachary had come to a breaking point, with no going back, only forward. Wherever that might take her. Consequently, Georgianna had nothing left to lose now but her pride. And where Zachary was concerned, she found that she now had none. How could she have, when she knew he had cast aside his own pride earlier this evening, by offering to get down on his knees and beg her forgiveness.

'The brandy, Hinds, if you please?' she reminded, sending Hinds scurrying down the hallway.

Zachary was dressed far less formally than he had

been earlier this evening, having removed his jacket and cravat, leaving him dressed only in his waistcoat over the snowy white shirt open at the throat and black pantaloons, which clearly showed the lean perfection of his muscled legs and thighs.

He looked delicious, Georgianna decided, good enough to eat, in fact. The heated colour warmed her cheeks as she recalled that she had already tasted and devoured Zachary, when the two of them made love together yesterday afternoon.

She held Zachary's wary gaze unwaveringly as she softly crossed the hallway to join him. 'May I come in?' she beseeched huskily, her heart beating erratically in her chest as he made no effort to stand aside and allow her entry into his study.

Zachary's hand tightened on the doorframe, where he had reached out to steady himself in his complete surprise at seeing Georgianna standing in the entrance hall of his London home. 'Is Jeffrey with you?'

'Jeffrey knows that I am here, because he put me into our carriage himself. Otherwise, I am quite alone,' she dismissed huskily.

A scowl darkened Zachary's brow. 'That was most improper of you.'

She gazed up at him quizzically. 'As you stated earlier, we are well past that point.'

Maybe so, but Zachary's concern was on Georgianna's behalf, rather than his own. His own reputation was such that her visiting him alone would only add to his reputation as being something of a rake, whereas Georgianna's still bore a question mark, as far as society was concerned.

'Why are you here, Georgianna?' he prompted warily.

'You would rather I had not come?'

He would far rather Georgianna stayed and never left. Ever again. But, as their earlier conversation had seemed to confirm that was not even a possibility, he could not help but question as to the reason why Georgianna had left the Countess of Evesham's ball only minutes after he had done so himself. With the intent, it seemed, of following him here. With her brother's full consent and co-operation, by the sound of it.

His mouth tightened disapprovingly. 'Jeffrey should have known better than to allow it.'

'Jeffrey overheard part of our own conversation on the terrace earlier.'

'I can see I shall have to have words with that young man regarding his habit of eavesdropping on private conversations.' Zachary scowled.

Georgianna shook her head. 'He is far more mature and sensible than either of us have given him credit for,' she assured drily. 'But would you rather I left again, Zachary?' She looked up at him searchingly.

He drew a deep breath into his starved lungs as he realised he had forgotten to breathe. He allowed himself to indulge his senses where Georgianna was concerned, gazing upon her obvious beauty and the dewy perfection of her skin, that begged to be touched and tasted, and now breathing in her unique perfume—

something floral as well as the unique and feminine warmth that was all Georgianna.

'I would rather you had not come here at all,' he maintained harshly, still making no effort to step aside and allow her entry to his study. It was his last bastion of defence, a place where he did not have any visible memories of being with Georgianna. Unlike his bedchamber upstairs. And the bedchamber adjoining that one. And the blue salon.

Her chin rose determinedly. 'I wished to continue our earlier conversation.'

His jaw tightened. 'And I believe we said then all that needs be said to each other.'

Georgianna looked up at Zachary searchingly, as she easily noted his unkempt appearance. His hair was tousled, as if he had run his agitated fingers through it several times since returning home. The lines beside his eyes and mouth seemed deeper, his mouth set in a thin and uncompromising line, and there was a dark shadow upon his jaw, where he was obviously in need of a second shave of the day.

Altogether, he looked nothing like the suave and sophisticated gentleman who had arrived at the Countess of Evesham's ball earlier this evening.

Because of the unsatisfactory outcome earlier of that conversation with her?

That was what Georgianna was here to find out. And, having made that decision, she had no intentions of leaving here tonight until she had done so.

'You know, Zachary, we both have scars that are visible to the eye if one cares to look for them.' Her gaze softened as she reached up to gently touch the livid scar upon his throat, stubbornly maintaining that touch even when he would have flinched away. 'But I, for one, have other scars, ones deep inside me, that are not at all visible to the naked eye.' She smiled sadly. 'They are the scars left by my unhappy experience at André's hands. Of uncertainty. Of questioning my self-worth.'

'The devil they are.'

Georgianna nodded as Zachary scowled his displeasure at her admission. 'Those scars make it difficult for me to believe that any man, any gentleman, could ever, would ever, want to be with me after—Zachary?' she questioned sharply as he reached up to curl his fingers about her wrist before pulling her inside his candlelit study and closing the door firmly behind them. His eyes were a dark, unfathomable grey as he gazed down at her hungrily before his arms moved about her and he lowered his head to crush her lips beneath his own.

It would have been so easy to lose herself in that kiss. For Georgianna to give in completely to the arousal which instantly thrummed through her body. To feel gratified, to revel, in this proof that Zachary still desired her, at least.

But she could not. Dared not. Because she knew it would be all too easy to give in to those desires and for the two of them not to talk at all. And they needed the truth between the two of them, before, or if, there was to be any more lovemaking.

Georgianna wrenched her mouth from beneath

Zachary's even as she pushed against his chest to free herself.

His arms fell reluctantly away as he stepped back, his heavy lidded gaze now guarded. 'I trust that answers your question as to whether or not you are wanted by me?'

She drew in a shaky breath, even more determined, after Zachary's show of passion, to say all the things she knew needed to be said between them. 'I made a mistake last year, Zachary, one for which so many people have suffered.'

'You most of all,' he pointed out gruffly.

She sighed equally as shakily. 'I really was so very young, and even more foolish. I am ashamed to say that at the time I saw it all as a grand adventure, with no real thought for what the long-term consequences of my actions might be.'

'Except to escape being married to me,' Zachary reminded drily.

'Yes.' Georgianna's gaze now avoided meeting his, as she began to pace the rug before the warmth of the fireplace. 'And now I have so many things to thank you for, Zachary.'

His eyes widened. 'What on earth…?'

'I am so grateful for your own efforts, last year and now, to maintain my reputation in society,' she continued determinedly. 'So thankful that Jeffrey has had you to help him through these trying months since our father died. And…' she looked up at him helplessly '…and, yes, I am more gratified than I have cared to admit, until now, that you have helped rid the world of a monster such as André Rousseau.' That last admission was against everything she had been brought up to believe in regard to the sanctity of human life.

It was also, Georgianna now accepted, a large part of why she had been so angry with Zachary when he had informed her of André's death. Because, having lived in fear of discovery by André these past few months, she had wanted him to be dead. Wished him so. And she had inwardly rejoiced yesterday when Zachary had told her André was indeed dead.

It was a reaction, a rejoicing, of which she had felt heartily ashamed.

But that shame and anger were directed towards herself, not Zachary. 'I was ashamed to admit it until now,' she admitted huskily.

'But you loved him. Love him still, damn it.'

Her eyes widened. 'I most certainly do not. I...' She paused, chewing briefly on her bottom lip before continuing. 'I fear I have been less than honest, with myself, and with you, on that matter.'

Zachary gave a grimace. 'Your reaction yesterday, your distress, were evidence enough of how you felt. That you still had feelings for the man,' he added harshly.

'No,' Georgianna denied vehemently. 'Never that. Never,' she repeated with a shudder of revulsion. 'The truth of the matter is—I realised some time ago—Zachary, I do not believe I was ever truly in love with André.' She gave a pained grimace at the admission. 'I was very naïve, flattered by his attentions and desperate to escape a loveless marriage and, I now know, in love with love rather than André himself.'

Zachary stared at her searchingly for long, tense moments, before turning abruptly to cross the room and seat himself behind his imposing mahogany desk. That she had not loved Rousseau after all was no reason to suppose, to hope, she would ever love him.

'I am gratified to you—' he nodded '—for allowing me to know that Rousseau's death has not succeeded in breaking your heart, as I previously believed it to have done.'

Georgianna could hear the *but* in his voice.

But the admission made no difference to the outcome of their own conversation, perhaps?

Whether or not that was true, Georgianna had no intentions of leaving here tonight without there being complete honesty between herself and Zachary. After which, fate, or rather Zachary, could do with her what it would. 'Are you not interested to know how it is I came to be certain I was never in love with André?'

His mouth twisted wryly. 'No doubt it is difficult to continue to love a man whom you knew had attempted to kill you.'

'Indeed.' She nodded ruefully. 'Almost as difficult, in fact, as finding you have fallen in love with the very same gentleman whose hand in marriage you had once shunned so cruelly.'

Zachary rose sharply to his feet. 'Georgianna?' His eyes glittered as he gazed across at her uncertainly.

Her heart was now beating so erratically, so loudly in her chest, she felt sure that Zachary could not help but be aware of it, too, despite the distance between them. 'It is the truth, Zachary.' She forced herself to forge ahead, to not retreat or back down, now that she had come so far. 'Since I returned to England you have shown me a side of yourself I did not know existed. That I did not even dare dream existed. On the outside you are so very much the cool and arrogant Duke of Hawksmere, so very much in control. But inwardly there is a kindness to you, one which you try to hide, but which shines through anyway.'

'And you reached this conclusion by my having locked you in my bedchamber? By my making love to you at every opportunity?' He raised incredulous brows.

'I reached that conclusion by knowing that you could have been so much harsher with me, after the way I had behaved in the past. By knowing that you were complicit in protecting my reputation, despite that behaviour. By your overwhelming kindness to Jeffrey these past months. And by the realisation this evening, the certainty,' she declared determinedly as he would have spoken, 'that your reasons for seeing André dispatched were not, as I had supposed, because of loyalty to England, or because of a personal grudge you held against him, for having dared to elope with your future bride.'

'Dear God, you thought that of me?'

Colour warmed the paleness of her cheeks. 'I am ashamed to say it occurred to me those might be your reasons.'

'I did it because of you, Georgianna. Because

André had attempted to kill you.' Zachary's hands were clenched at his side.

It was as Georgianna had thought earlier when he'd pleaded with her so emotionally.

'Just leave it on the side table there,' Zachary instructed his butler harshly as the man entered after the briefest of knocks, holding aloft the tray with the decanter and glasses. 'And in future, would you please knock and wait before entering any room in which Lady Georgianna and I are alone together?' he added, his gaze remaining intent upon Georgianna.

'Certainly, your Grace.' The butler placed the tray upon the side table. 'Will that be all, your Grace?'

Zachary barely resisted the impulse to tell the man to go to the devil, wishing to be alone again with Georgianna, to continue their conversation. To hear her repeat that she had fallen in love with him.

Something he hardly dared to believe.

'You may retire for the night, Hinds,' Zachary dismissed distractedly. 'And thank you.'

His butler gave him another startled glance before gathering himself and leaving the room. As evidence perhaps that Zachary's temper had been less than pleasant this past few days?

As no doubt it had, caught up in the pained whirlpool of his uncertainty in his own emotions, as he had surely been.

'Is that not a strange request to make of your butler, when there is no reason to suppose that the two of us might ever be alone together in a room in this house again?' Georgianna queried huskily.

Zachary stepped out from behind his desk. 'There is every reason to suppose it, Georgianna.' He strode purposefully towards her before grasping both of her hands in his. 'Believe me, when I tell you, that these past three weeks I have come to love and admire you beyond anything and anyone else in this world.'

'Zachary?' she choked out emotionally.

'Georgia, will you please, I beg of you, consent to becoming my wife?'

Georgianna stared up at him wonderingly, sure Zachary could not truly have told her that he loved her, too. That he had begged her to marry him?

His hands tightened about hers as he obviously mistook her silence for hesitation. 'And not because of any ridiculous clause in my father's will, either. Indeed, if you require it as proof of the sincerity of my feelings for you, I will give away half of the Hawksmere fortune to my cousin Rufus forthwith, as my father's will decrees if I do not have an heir by my thirty fifth birthday. Anything, if you will consent to become my wife immediately.'

Georgianna's mouth felt very dry, and after its wild pounding earlier she was sure her heart had now ceased to beat altogether. 'Is your cousin in need of half the Hawksmere fortune?'

'Thanks to Rufus's business acumen, he is already one of the richest men in London.' Zachary bared his teeth in a brief smile before just as quickly sobering. 'Nevertheless, I will happily give him the money, if it will ensure that you believe I am sincere in my declaration of love for you. If you will only consent to become my wife as soon as it can be arranged?'

Georgianna had no idea what she had expected the outcome of her visit here this evening to be, but she knew she had certainly never expected it to be the complete and utter happiness of hearing Hawksmere declare his love for her and his asking her to marry him.

Her vision was blurred by those tears of happiness. 'You truly love me?'

'To the point of madness,' Zachary assured fervently. 'Indeed, I believe I have been half-insane with the emotion these past few days.' The intensity of his gaze held her. 'I love you so very much, Georgianna Rose Lancaster.'

'As I love you, Zachary Richard Edward Black,' she answered him huskily. 'Completely. And always.'

His face lit up. 'Then put all of the past behind us and consent to marry me.'

She swallowed. 'Are you absolutely sure that is what you want, Zachary? My reappearance in society is still tenuous.'

'What are you suggesting, Georgianna?' Zachary demanded. 'That I should make you my mistress rather than marry you? That I should hide you away somewhere?'

'I am something of a novelty in society just now, Zachary, but if anyone should ever learn of my elopement with André…'

'They will not discover it,' Zachary announced arrogantly. 'And even if they did, none would dare to question the reputation of the Duchess of Hawksmere.'

It was a name, a title, when used in connection to herself, that had once filled Georgianna with such dread. Now it only filled her with a happiness that threatened to overwhelm her. 'I am so in love with you, Zachary. So very, very much, my darling. And if you are serious in your proposal of marriage…?'

'I will accept nothing less,' he assured firmly.

She glowed up at him. 'Then I believe I should much prefer that you keep the Hawksmere fortune intact for our children, when they are born.'

'Georgianna?' Zachary had almost been afraid to hope, to dream, that Georgianna would ever accept his proposal. 'You truly will consent to become my wife?' His fingers tightened painfully about hers. 'You will marry me as soon as a special licence can be arranged?'

She nodded happily. 'And Jeffrey shall give me away and one of your friends, Wolfingham, perhaps, shall stand up with you. Oh, yes, I will marry you, Zachary. Yes, yes, please, yes.' She launched herself into his arms as his mouth swooped down to once again claim hers.

'You were very brave to come here alone this evening, my love,' Zachary murmured admiringly some time later, Georgianna's head resting on his chest as the two of them lay on the chaise in his study together. He played with her curls, having once again released her hair so that it cascaded loosely down her back.

She laughed softly, contentedly, the two of them having professed their love for each other over and over again this past hour or more. 'To confront the fierce lion in his den?'

'To have completely tamed the lion in his den,' Zachary corrected with humour. 'Indeed, I find I am so much in love with you I very much doubt I shall ever be able to deny you anything in future, love.'

Georgianna hesitated, knowing that there was still one thing that she had not confessed to her beloved. The last confession.

When she first returned to England she had been too angry at Hawksmere's incarceration of her, to talk of such things, and since then there had been no right time, no opportunity, for her to do so.

'What is it, Georgia?' Zachary sat up slightly as he sensed her sudden tension. His hands gently cupped either side of her face as he looked down at her searchingly. 'Tell me, my love.'

She chewed on her bottom lip. 'I— It is only— A lady should not talk of such things,' she choked out emotionally.

'Now you are seriously worrying me, love.' Zachary frowned. 'We have talked about so much this past hour. The past, the now, our future together. What on earth is there that still bothers you so much that you look as if you are about to cry?'

Georgianna felt as if she were about to cry. It was all too embarrassing. Too humiliating.

Her gaze dropped from his as she moistened her

lips with the tip of her tongue. 'When I eloped with André...'

'I thought we had agreed earlier that we would not discuss that ever again,' Zachary reminded with chiding gentleness.

'Just this one thing, Zachary,' she pleaded. 'It is important, if we are to be married.'

'We are most certainly going to be married and sooner rather than later.' Zachary had never been as happy as he had felt this past hour of knowing that Georgianna loved him, that she had consented to marry him. He could not bear it if that happiness— if a lifetime with Georgianna as his wife, should ever be snatched away from him.

'Whatever you have yet to tell me, never doubt my love for you, Georgianna. Never. Do you under-stand?' He held her tightly against him. 'Be assured, nothing you have to say, now or in the future, will ever change that,' he added with certainty.

Georgianna looked up at him wonderingly, moved beyond measure at the knowledge that Zachary loved her so deeply, so unconditionally. The same deep in-tensity of emotion with which she now loved him. 'It is nothing bad, my love,' she assured huskily as she reached up to stroke his cheek. 'Only embarrassing for me to speak of,' she conceded ruefully.

'I grow more intrigued by the moment, my love.' He eyed her quizzically.

'Where to start?' Georgianna pulled out of his arms before standing up and turning away slightly, her hands clasped tightly together in front of her.

'When I eloped with André—allow me to finish, my love, please!' she begged as Zachary made a noise of protest. 'We spent several uncomfortable days being jostled about in the coach together on the way to the seaport. We passed the sea journey as brother and sister in separate cabins. And once we reached Paris…' She gave a shake of her head. 'You are well aware of what transpired within days of our reaching the French capital.'

Zachary's narrowed gaze remained intently on Georgianna as he slowly stood up to move softly to her side, reaching down to lift her chin so that he might gaze down directly, searchingly, into the frankness of those violet-coloured eyes. 'Are you saying…?' He drew in a sharp breath, hardly daring to believe.

'I am saying that André and I had never shared any more than a few chaste kisses before we eloped and that he did not so much as kiss me during the whole of our journey to France.'

'Georgianna?'

She swallowed. 'The intensity, depth, of our own lovemaking was—is, the first I have ever known.'

'Can it be? Are you a virgin still, Georgianna?' Zachary prompted tensely.

The colour deepened in her cheeks as she nodded. 'I could not bear to tell you before now.' She grasped tightly to the front of his waistcoat as she gazed up at him imploringly. 'The Zachary I met on my return to England would have enjoyed tormenting me with that knowledge. Would have mocked and taunted me as to André's disinterest in me. Would have—'

'Hush, my love.' Zachary placed a silencing fingertip against her lips, his heart having swelled almost to bursting point in his chest.

He had long ago accepted that Georgianna had been Rousseau's lover and it had made no difference to the deep love and admiration, respect, that he now felt for her. But to now realise, to know, that Georgianna had never, would never, belong to any other man but him?

It was a priceless gift. A gift beyond anything Zachary might ever have imagined.

'I took such liberties with you.' He groaned, disgusted with himself. 'I was far too rough in my lovemaking. Too advanced in the things I did to you and demanded from you in return.'

'I loved the way you made love to me, Zachary, and so enjoyed making love to you,' she admitted shyly. 'Indeed, I cannot wait to repeat it.'

'That will not happen until after we are married,' he assured her determinedly.

She chuckled throatily. 'Can it be that Zachary Black, the arrogant and haughty Duke of Hawksmere, has now become prim and respectable?'

'You may take it that Zachary Black, the arrogant and haughty Duke of Hawksmere,' he repeated huskily, 'intends to cherish and love, to make love to, Georgianna Rose Black, Duchess of Hawksmere, and only Georgianna Rose Black, Duchess of Hawksmere, for the rest of their lives together.'

It was so much more, so indescribably, wonderfully, ecstatically more than Georgianna Rose Lancaster, soon to be Black, could ever have hoped or dreamed of.

* * * * *

Don't miss the next book in
Carole Mortimer's dazzling
DANGEROUS DUKES *duet:*
DARIAN HUNTER: DUKE OF DESIRE
Coming November 2014!

REQUEST YOUR FREE BOOKS!

 HARLEQUIN® HISTORICAL:
Where love is timeless

2 FREE NOVELS PLUS 2 FREE GIFTS!

YES! Please send me 2 FREE Harlequin® Historical novels and my 2 FREE gifts (gifts are worth about $10). After receiving them, if I don't wish to receive any more books, I can return the shipping statement marked "cancel." If I don't cancel, I will receive 6 brand-new novels every month and be billed just $5.44 per book in the U.S. or $5.74 per book in Canada. That's a savings of at least 16% off the cover price! It's quite a bargain! Shipping and handling is just 50¢ per book in the U.S. and 75¢ per book in Canada.* I understand that accepting the 2 free books and gifts places me under no obligation to buy anything. I can always return a shipment and cancel at any time. Even if I never buy another book, the two free books and gifts are mine to keep forever.

246/349 HDN F4ZY

Name	(PLEASE PRINT)	
Address		Apt. #
City	State/Prov.	Zip/Postal Code

Signature (if under 18, a parent or guardian must sign)

Mail to the **Harlequin® Reader Service:**
IN U.S.A.: P.O. Box 1867, Buffalo, NY 14240-1867
IN CANADA: P.O. Box 609, Fort Erie, Ontario L2A 5X3

Want to try two free books from another line?
Call 1-800-873-8635 or visit www.ReaderService.com.

* Terms and prices subject to change without notice. Prices do not include applicable taxes. Sales tax applicable in N.Y. Canadian residents will be charged applicable taxes. Offer not valid in Quebec. This offer is limited to one order per household. Not valid for current subscribers to Harlequin Historical books. All orders subject to credit approval. Credit or debit balances in a customer's account(s) may be offset by any other outstanding balance owed by or to the customer. Please allow 4 to 6 weeks for delivery. Offer available while quantities last.

Your Privacy—The Harlequin® Reader Service is committed to protecting your privacy. Our Privacy Policy is available online at www.ReaderService.com or upon request from the Harlequin Reader Service.

We make a portion of our mailing list available to reputable third parties that offer products we believe may interest you. If you prefer that we not exchange your name with third parties, or if you wish to clarify or modify your communication preferences, please visit us at www.ReaderService.com/consumerschoice or write to us at Harlequin Reader Service Preference Service, P.O. Box 9062, Buffalo, NY 14269. Include your complete name and address.

*An unexpected visitor transforms Christmas in the
Marsh household with a touch of much-needed
festive cheer...*

Read on for a sneak preview of Christine Merrill's
THE CHRISTMAS DUCHESS.

They moved on to the parlor, piling the mantel with
holly and ivy.

He glanced down at her. "You are smiling again,
Mrs. Marsh. Twice in one day. It must truly be Christmas."

Was it really so rare a thing to see her smile? She hoped
not. But now that he had commented on it, she could not
manage to raise the corners of her lips to prove him wrong.

The duke sighed. "And now it is gone again. Do you
think if we put up a kissing bough it will come back?"

"Certainly not." At least he had given her a reason to
frown. All the kindness in the world did not give him the
right to tease her.

"You have several fine arches, and a hook in the center
of the parlor where you might hang it." He glanced up in
mock sadness at the empty door frames. "And yet, I see
none there."

"That is because there is no point in hanging something
of that kind in this house," she said firmly, as though the
matter was settled. "There is no one here that wants or
needs kissing."

"Really," he said, surprised.

"My son is too young to care. If I allow my daughter to run riot I will have even more trouble than I do already. The servants have no right to be distracted with it for half the month of December."

"And you?" he prompted.

"I?" She did her best to pretend that the thought had not occurred to her. She turned away. "It is foolishness, and I have no time for that, either."

"Perhaps it is time to make the time," he said, stepping forward, holding the branch above her head and kissing her on the lips before she could object.

It was as if the world had been spinning at a mad rate and suddenly stopped, leaving her vision unnaturally clear. She was not a minor character waiting in the wings of her own life. She was standing in the center of the stage, alone except for the duke.

And then it was over. A strange, adolescent awkwardness fell over them. He cleared his throat. She straightened her skirt. They both glanced at the door and then back to each other. "I trust I have demonstrated the need for further decoration?" he said.

Christine Merrill's THE CHRISTMAS DUCHESS is one of three short stories in our Christmas anthology **WISH UPON A SNOWFLAKE.**

Available from Harlequin Historical November 2014, wherever books and ebooks are sold.

HISTORICAL

Where love is timeless

COMING IN NOVEMBER 2014

The Wrong Cowboy
by Lauri Robinson

One mail-order bride in need of rescue!

All the rigorous training in the world could not have prepared nursemaid Marie Hall for trailing the wilds of Dakota with six orphans. Especially when her ingenious plan—to pose as the mail-order bride of the children's next of kin—leads Marie to the *wrong* cowboy!

Proud and stubborn, Stafford Burleson is everything Marie's been taught to avoid. But with her fate and that of the children in his capable hands, Marie soon feels there's something incredibly *right* about this rugged rancher and his brooding charm….

Available wherever books and ebooks are sold.

HH29808

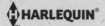
HARLEQUIN®

HISTORICAL

Where love is timeless

COMING IN NOVEMBER 2014

Darian Hunter: Duke of Desire
by Carole Mortimer

The Players:

Darian Hunter, Duke of Wolfingham: legendary rake
and notorious bachelor

Mariah Beecham, Countess of Carlisle: society's scandalous widow
and secret agent of the crown

The Stage:

A notoriously debauched house party

The Scene:

Forced to pose as lovers, Darian and Mariah must work
together to stop an assassination plot

The Twist:

As the shocking and oh-so-sensual games play out around
them, the romantic ruse becomes all too real. And the
tantalizing temptation to indulge their *every* desire
becomes overwhelming…

Available wherever books and ebooks are sold.

HISTORICAL

Where love is timeless

COMING IN NOVEMBER 2014

The Rake's Bargain
by Lucy Ashford

The stage is set

Deborah O'Hara loves her life leading her troupe of actors.
But when she becomes entangled in a web of secrets spun
by the rakishly handsome Damian Beaumaris,
Duke of Cirencester, she is forced to play the hardest role
of her life: that of the stunning but disloyal Paulette, the
duke's widowed sister-in-law.

To regain the honor of his family, Beau needs Deb's help.
But despite his intentions to let nothing distract him from his
plan, he doesn't bargain on the forbidden sparks that fly with
his beautiful leading lady....

Available wherever books and ebooks are sold.

JUST CAN'T GET ENOUGH?

Join our social communities
and talk to us online.

You will have access to the latest
news on upcoming titles and special
promotions, but most importantly,
you can talk to other fans about your
favorite Harlequin reads.

Harlequin.com/Community

 Facebook.com/HarlequinBooks

Twitter.com/HarlequinBooks

 Pinterest.com/HarlequinBooks